BOOK FOUR   HALEN

T.O. SMITH

Halen

SAVAGE CROWS MC MOTHER CHARTER
BOOK FOUR

For Riley, my reason for everything that I do.

For those of you who followed me to Amazon from Inkitt, you guys are absolutely amazing.

And for those of you who read the original Savage Crows MC series and decided to continue reading with the mother charter series, thank you!

©February 2022. T.O. Smith. All rights reserved.

No part of this book may be reproduced, distributed, or transmitted in any form or by any means, including photocopying, recording, or other electronic or mechanical systems, without written permission from the author, except for the use of brief quotations in a book review.

This book is a work of fiction. Names, characters, places, and incidents are either a product of the author's imagination or are used fictitiously, and any resemblance to actual persons, living or dead, events, or locales is entirely coincidental.

Cover Design: Tiff Writes Romance

Editing: Tiff Writes Romance

Proofreading: Kimberly Peterson, Taylor Jade

BOOKS IN THE SERIES

Brett - Book One

Kyle - Book Two

Damon - Book Three

Halen - Book Four

Logan - Book Five

Walker - Book Six

Vincent - Book Seven

SAVAGE CROWS MOTHER CHARTER

Copper - President
Damon - Vice President
Kyle - Road Captain
Halen - Sergeant at Arms
Vincent - Enforcer
Brett - Secretary
Logan - Treasurer
Walker - Chaplain

SAVAGE CROWS (TX CHARTER)

Blink: Founder
Grim: President
Alex: Vice President
Ink: Road Captain
Hatchet: Sergeant at Arms
Thor: Enforcer
Grave: Secretary
Bullet: Treasurer
Sabotage: Chaplain
Scab: Patch

SIDE NOTES

A chaplain is normally the one over all of the spiritual things in a club, as well as performs marriage ceremonies, funerals, and puts protection on members in jail.

A chaplain in my book is the one the members go to for advice. So, please keep that in mind while reading this book.

Thanks!

CHAPTER ONE
HALEN

"Uncle Halen, why do I have to get my teeth cleaned?" Jayla asked me from the backseat of my truck. I rolled my eyes to the roof for a moment, begging for some patience. Between Ryker and Jayla - Copper and Penny's twins - Jayla was the most inquisitive one, and she had to have an answer for *everything*.

"Because the dentist has to make sure that all of your teeth are white and pretty," I told her, silently thanking God that her school was just up ahead. So far, I'd had to explain to her why the grass is green, why some patches of grass might be brown, and why trees grew so tall.

I glanced at the little blonde in my rearview mirror. She was frowning in thoughtfulness. "If the dentist does that for me, then why do I have to brush my teeth?"

God, grant me patience, I pleaded.

"Because if you wait for the dentist to clean your teeth every six months, they'll fall out," I bluntly told her, turning into the entrance of her elementary school.

Her eyes widened in horror. "Oh, God!" she exclaimed. Her hands flew to her mouth, and I had to resist the urge to laugh. She was so much like her mother that it was insane. "I need my teeth, Uncle Halen!"

"Then, continue brushing them," I told her. I slid out of my truck and walked around to the backdoor to open it for her. I lifted her down and grabbed her hand in mine, walking her into the school.

"Bubba is going to be so mad that I got to miss some of school and he didn't," Jayla suddenly said.

I snorted. "Then, you tell him if he doesn't like it, he can take it up with Uncle Halen," I assured her. I pushed open the door to the front office, smiling at the receptionist sitting at the desk.

"Hi, checking in a student?" she asked me.

"Yeah." I pulled the note from the dentist from my pocket, sliding it across to her. "Jayla had a dentist appointment."

Jayla smiled at the receptionist. "Hi, Mrs. Newman."

Mrs. Newman smiled at Jayla. "Hi, Jayla. Was the dentist appointment okay?"

Jayla nodded. "I found out if I don't brush my teeth every day, then they'll all fall out."

I barked a laugh. Even Mrs. Newman looked amused. "Alright, Mr. Anderson. She's signed in. I'll walk her to class."

I knelt and pressed a kiss to the top of Jayla's head. "Be good," I told her as I adjusted the straps on her backpack. "Remember what I told you to tell Ryker if he gives you a hard time."

She nodded. "You'll beat him up," she said in all seriousness.

I shot her a deadpan look. She grinned, giggling as she did so. "I know, Uncle Halen. Tell him he has you to deal with if he doesn't like that I got to miss school."

I poked her nose, smiling at her. She giggled. "Good girl. I'll see you this evening, yeah?" I shot her a stern look. "And be good for your mom when she comes to pick you up."

She nodded. "Yes, sir."

Yeah, there was a slim chance she and Ryker would behave for Penny, but fuck, I tried.

I walked out of the front office and to my truck. An older, red Toyota was parked behind it, and a woman whom I presumed was a teacher was packing some boxes into it, sniffling as tears ran down her cheeks.

She was pretty as fuck. Her white-blonde hair fell down her back in soft, natural waves, and those brown eyes of hers were extremely beautiful despite them being bloodshot from crying so much.

And fuck, those curves under that pencil skirt she was wearing?

Fuck. Me.

"Do you need some help?" I asked her.

She jerked her head up to stare at me in astonishment. Her eyes widened even further as she took in all of my tattoos and the cut that labeled me as the Sergeant at Arms of the Savage Crows MC.

She quickly swiped at her cheeks. "No," she croaked. I smiled at her as she cleared her throat. God, she was even prettier now that she was facing me. "I just lost my job - that's all."

I frowned at her. "Name's Halen," I said, introducing myself. "You want to grab a coffee?" I asked her. "My treat," I quickly added when she shot me a look that clearly said '*really*'. "Most of the women in my life like donuts and coffee when they're feeling down."

"Seriously?" she snapped. "Most of the women in your life? Are you serious right now?"

I sighed, quickly realizing that came out completely wrong. "Sorry," I quickly apologized. I gestured to my cut. "My brothers' wives," I explained. "Donuts and coffee from Rosanna's normally help them cheer up a bit."

She relaxed at my words. I resisted the urge to smirk. This woman was a fucking spitfire, and I couldn't wait to tame her.

"Coffee sounds perfect," she said quietly. "And, um, my name is Genesis. I'm sorry for being so snappy. Things are just—"

"Hey, take it easy." I grabbed a box and put it in her trunk. "I'll help you get the rest of this put in your car, and then, we can go grab a coffee. Sound like a plan?"

She gave me a small smile that caused a strange tingling sensation in the pit of my stomach. "Sounds like a great plan."

"So, what happened to get you fired?" I asked her as she sipped at her coffee.

She sighed, looking troubled. "There's a student in my class that I'm extremely concerned about." I nodded at her to continue. "There are clear signs of abuse, but no one will listen to me, and he never has money for lunch. The poor child looks like he's being starved." I clenched my jaw. "So, I buy him his lunch every day, and today, the principal pulled me into his office, claimed that I was taking advantage of a child, and fired me."

Anger simmered in my gut, but I didn't say anything. But I did make a mental note to call my brother who worked at the Department of Family and Children Services as an investigator for these kinds of situations and have him dig something up.

I would be taking this kid in as soon as he was removed. I had a soft spot for mistreated children.

Both my brother and I had been victims of child abuse.

The only difference between us was that my brother went to therapy and college and turned our shitty childhood into something good.

I went a destructive route, and Copper found me strung out, getting my ass kicked for running my mouth. He put mc through rehab and then allowed me to prospect for the club.

My phone went off. I shot Genesis a sheepish look as I pulled it out of my pocket.

Copper.

"Yeah," I said when I answered.

"Well, don't you sound fucking chipper." I grunted. "Need you at the clubhouse this evening," he told me. "We've got a run coming up, and I need you with us for this one."

"Got it," I told him. "I'll be there."

I hung up. Genesis frowned at her watch. "I need to head home," she told me. She was using my phone call as her escape, but I didn't say anything. "Thank you for the coffee and donuts." She gave me that small smile again. "They actually did help a little."

I smiled at her. "Happy to be of service."

She stood, grabbing her purse from the back of the chair. "Thank you again, Halen."

I nodded at her as she slipped away from the table, scampering towards her car. It was clear I made her nervous, but I had no intention of leaving that woman alone.

I wanted her.

But first, I had other things to take care of - like calling my brother and seeing if he could find out anything from the school about that student.

"Did she give you a name for this kid?" Drake asked me as he typed in the number for the school.

I shook my head, glancing out the slim window of his office that looked out onto the parking lot. "No. And I didn't ask. Figured if she didn't give it, then it meant she couldn't say."

Drake nodded, putting his finger up to me as he connected with someone. "Hi, yes. I need to speak to one of your guidance counselors. My name is Drake Anderson, and I'm with the Department of Family and Children Services." He paused for a moment. "Yes, I can hold."

"If they ask who you got your information from, give them my name," I told him. He looked up at me. "She already lost her job over this. I don't want her facing more backlash."

He nodded in understanding. "Hi, yes. My name is Drake Anderson. I'm with DFCS, and I'm calling with concerns for a student at your school."

I walked around his office, looking at the diplomas that he had hanging on his office walls. My brother had truly made something of himself, and he was making a difference in the lives of kids in this town.

"Yes. I had a gentleman come into my office today informing me that he overheard a conversation about a teacher losing her job over trying to help a child. He wanted to make an official report and have me look into it." He paused. "Of course - understandable. The teacher's first name is . . ." he paused again, looking up at me.

"Genesis," I told him. I'd already told him that, but Drake had a way of doing things that I didn't understand.

"Genesis," Drake repeated. "He doesn't know her last name. As I stated before, he overheard the conversation." He looked at his watch. "Yes, I can come in today. I'll be there in thirty minutes. I appreciate your cooperation."

He hung up and stood from his desk, looking at me. "I'll give you a call if I remove the child from the home," he told me. "You're still up to date as a foster parent in our system?"

"You know it," I told him. I made sure to continue the inspections of my home and everything else that came with being a foster parent for this exact reason.

"And you're sure you want to take this kid on?" he asked me.

I nodded. "Drake, if it's possible, I might adopt him," I admitted. "But we'll cross that bridge when we get to it." I pulled my truck keys from my pocket. "I need to head into the shop for a few hours. Keep me informed."

I walked out of his office, shooting a smile at Mrs. Evelyn, the gray-haired receptionist. "Have a good day, Mrs. Evelyn."

"You, too, hun!" she called, waving her weathered hand at me from behind her desk.

I stepped outside and groaned as I looked at my watch, realizing I was already thirty minutes late for work. I was supposed to have been in at one, and it was already one-thirty.

Kyle was going to have my ass if Olivia didn't first, but oh, well.

Some things were just a bit more important.

CHAPTER TWO
GENESIS

I frowned at the notice on my door. I had one week to get my landlord all of the back owed rent on my measly little apartment, or I could kiss having a home goodbye.

Problem was, no schools would hire me. Every time that my old school was called to verify my employment history, they bad-mouthed me and made me out to basically be a pedophile, a child molester.

All I had tried to do was *take care* of a child. That was it. He had needed *help*. And since no one would fucking believe me, I took matters into my own hands.

And it had backfired – blew up right in my face.

With a sigh, I closed my apartment door, ripping the notice off and shoving it into my purse as I did so. Then, I marched down the creaky stairs to my car to begin looking around for more work. Even if it was just part-time and I had to work three jobs, then that's what I would do.

Desperate times called for desperate measures.

The first place I passed was Frazier's – a mechanic and body shop in town. Their first location was on the other side of town, near the motorcycle club. I actually remembered this one being opened and all of the construction that had been at the site for months as they built the garage to Kyle Frazier's standards.

They currently had a sign out front on their fence advertising that they were hiring for a receptionist position.

I knew Kyle Frazier paid decently, and he was well known around town, so he got a hell of a lot of business, hence his need for a second location. It was mostly just the local MC guys that worked at the two shops, but occasionally, Kyle would hire outside of the club, too.

I was hoping that I could get lucky and secure a job there today.

What I didn't expect to see was Halen sliding out from beneath a truck, grease smeared on his cheek and covering his hands. He looked sinfully hot in a dark-gray pair of coveralls and steel-toed boots with a black bandana wrapped around his forehead to catch sweat.

"Can I help you?" a gruff voice asked to the side of me.

I looked over to see an older guy, probably in his late thirties, wiping his hands on a grease towel. He had tattoos covering his body from head to toe, and he honestly put me on edge.

"Damon, stop scaring people," Kyle said as he stepped out of the office. "How many times do I have to tell you to stop talking to customers when they come in?"

Damon shot him a look that would have scared me out of my wits if I'd been on the receiving end of it, but Kyle just shook his head and moved towards me, holding his hand out. "Kyle Frazier. How can I help you?"

I gestured towards the fence. "I saw that you're hiring, and I'm in desperate need of a job."

He nodded with a relieved grin. "Come on into the office. I'll go ahead and have you fill out an application, and I'll do an on-the-spot interview."

"Hey, Kyle, let me talk to you for a minute while she's filling that out," Halen called as he rolled back under the truck he was working on. "Need to talk to you about this damn truck."

"Got it," Kyle told him before he led me into the office, shutting the door behind us. "Normally, my wife helps manage the office here, but she likes to get her hands dirty in the garage, and being in an office drives her a bit stir crazy," he explained. I'd seen a woman working here when I passed by sometimes, but I hadn't realized she was his wife. Kind of fit though.

Kyle set a two-page application on the desk. "Take a seat." He put a pen on the application. "Go ahead and fill this out. I'll be back in a few minutes."

He slipped out of the office, leaving me alone. I sat down and grabbed the pen. The application was extremely simple, nothing like I normally had been filling out for teaching positions. It was simple and straight to the chase. I didn't even see a spot for employment history, which I found strange.

The rest of the application wasn't even information about me. It was simple math and reading questions, probably just to make sure I had enough of a brain to manage the office and the paperwork.

Honestly, after being a teacher for almost five years, I felt like managing an office would be simple as hell.

Managing eight and nine-year-olds could be fucking torture on most days.

Kyle came back into the office right as I finished answering the last question. He shot me an easy-going smile as I handed him the application. "You're hired," he told me. I gaped at him. "Halen said he knew you and put in a good word for you." I scowled. *Of course*. Don't get me wrong; I was grateful I had a job, but I had a feeling Halen wanted in my fucking pants. I'd made it a mission to avoid the man ever since we'd had coffee together.

There was something about him that was completely different from other men I had dated. He had a way of making my heart race and butterflies erupt in my gut.

It wasn't *normal*.

"Pay starts out at thirteen an hour. Prove to me you're damn good at what you do and pay bumps up to sixteen. Sound good?"

My eyes widened, Halen momentarily forgotten. "Thirteen?" I squeaked. "Sixteen?"

He laughed at my stupefied expression and nodded. "I make a shit ton of money running these two garages. I know I wouldn't be here without my employees, so I make sure to pay everyone decently, give bonuses, and also offer great benefits, which you'll begin to receive after your first initial thirty days."

I was blown away. *Holy shit.* I'd expected minimum wage – not thirteen fucking dollars an hour. I wouldn't even need a second or third job.

"Um, when do I start?" I asked him.

"Can you be here tomorrow at eight? We don't open until nine, but I try to make sure all of my employees are at the shop an hour before opening so we have time to get our shit together before the day starts."

"Eight is fine," I assured him. For thirteen a fucking hour, six A.M. would have been fine.

"And overtime is double – not time and a half," he informed me. He reached across the desk to shake my hand, and I quickly stuck it out. "I need to go help Damon, but I look forward to having you as an employee, Genesis."

He stepped out of the office. Halen stepped inside after Kyle walked out. I clenched my jaw, glaring at him. "What's your end goal here?" I demanded right off the bat. Halen simply arched an eyebrow at me, which only pissed me off. "What - you want sex?" I demanded. "Tough fucking luck, Halen. You won't be getting any."

He barked out a laugh that grated on my fucking nerves. "Sex would be fucking fantastic, don't get me wrong, but that's not why I told Kyle to hire you." I gaped at him, not expecting him to have been so blunt. "If you're still looking for a job after a month of losing your teaching position, then you're obviously desperate to have some kind of employment. Kyle pays fucking well; I'd have been stupid to not get him to hire you."

He grabbed a set of keys from the wall. "You up for a drive? I want to show you something."

"We're not having sex," I told him.

He grinned at me. "Baby, we will one day, but not today." *Oh, my God.* "Just come on. You'll enjoy this surprise."

I doubted it, but my stupid ass followed him anyway.

CHAPTER THREE
HALEN

Genesis frowned over at me. "The only thing on this side of town is the school." Then, she scowled. I wanted to laugh. I knew this woman would forever keep me on my toes if I could just figure out a way to get her to warm up to me. "Are you playing some kind of joke on me right now, Halen?" she snapped.

I shook my head at her. "No," I assured her. I knew taking her by the school on a drive to tease her would hurt her. I could be an asshole, but even I had my limits. "I can be a dick, but I wouldn't ever do that to you." I reached over and gently squeezed her thigh, my cock hardening in my jeans at the feeling of that soft thigh beneath my palm. God, I couldn't wait to hold those thighs open as I slid my cock deep inside of her. Her breath hitched in her throat at my touch. "Just trust me."

"Hard to do that when I barely know you, Halen," she retorted.

"My full name is Halen Anderson. I'm thirty-four years old, and I'm the Sergeant at Arms of the local motorcycle club. I own my home, this truck, and my bike – no more payments needed." She gaped at me. "If you run a background check on me, you'll see that I was arrested numerous times for drugs and public disturbances. You *might* find that I was shoved into rehab about ten years ago as well. Been clean ever since." I pulled into the parking lot of the school and opened my truck door. "And my brother is Drake Johnson. He works for the Department of Family and Children Services." I pointed my finger at her. "Stay."

Her face went from stunned to angry within a split second. "What the fuck am I – a dog?" she demanded.

I smirked at her. God, she was hell on wheels. "Nah, babe. Just sit tight, will you?"

I closed the door and walked into the school. Just as I had wanted, as soon as Randall had been removed from his dad, he had come to live with me, and for now, I was his foster parent, though I was currently in the process of working with the state to get his dad's rights to him revoked so that I could officially adopt him.

After taking him to see a doctor and a therapist a few times right after getting him, I'd come to find out that Randall actually suffered from Autism. He wasn't very high on the spectrum, but certain things set him off.

For example, ever since I had gotten him, I had walked him into school every morning all the way to his classroom, and every day after school, I picked him up from his classroom. We had tried not doing it one day, and he'd had a meltdown. The only thing that had calmed him down was the smell of my leather cut of all things.

His therapist said it probably reminded him of me, which was his safety.

I smiled at Randall as soon as the little boy came into view. Randall immediately turned into a little ball of energy, and he rushed towards me, wrapping his arms around me. "Hi, Dad."

Randall had also taken to calling me Dad now that I was his parent. The therapist hadn't been too sure about it at first, but when we had suggested him calling me Halen, he'd clammed up.

So, Dad, it was.

"Hey, kiddo. You ready to go? I have a surprise for you. I think you'll really like this one."

He beamed up at me. "Really?" God, this kid was so trusting of me. "Let's go!"

I grabbed his hand in mine and led him back out to my truck where Genesis was still waiting, though she looked a bit aggravated to be sitting in my truck by herself for that long. As soon as I opened the backdoor and Randall climbed in, his eyes got wide with excitement. "Ms. Genesis!" Randall exclaimed.

Genesis turned in her seat so quickly that I was surprised she didn't hurt her neck. "Randall?" she whispered in astonishment. She looked at me, and tears immediately flooded her eyes. "Oh, sweetheart, you're okay!" she exclaimed.

I grinned and shut the door, walking around to the driver's side so I could take us to the clubhouse. "I live with Dad now," Randall told her, referring to me. "He has a really big house, and I have a big Pitbull, too. Dad says he's there to keep me safe."

Genesis blinked over at me, tears sliding down her cheeks. "You – you believed me?" she choked out.

Oh, God. This woman crying over my little boy was going to do my heart in.

I nodded. "I come from some rough shit, babe. The moment you told me about him, I went to my brother. Randall has been in my care for almost a month now," I told her.

"Thank you." She sniffled. "I've been so worried about him."

I reached over and grabbed her hand, gently squeezing my fingers around hers. "No reason to be anymore," I assured her. "He's safe, and he's in good hands, not to mention, he's surrounded by a bunch of uncles and doting aunties. He's thriving."

She squeezed my hand in return before she let go, turning slightly in her seat to face Randall. He talked a mile a minute to her, which I was really glad to see. He still clammed up some at the clubhouse around the other guys, but once they talked to him enough, they managed to coax him out of his shell.

But Randall obviously adored Genesis, which was even more of a reason to keep her around.

This woman was fucking perfect for me. I just needed her to understand that I was damn close to being perfect for her, too.

Once we got to the clubhouse, I sent Randall inside to go ahead and get his homework set out so he could begin working on it. It was a routine we always had. As soon as I had explained to everyone what was going on with Randall, how I was taking him in and planning to adopt him, Kyle had rearranged my work shift so I could take Randall to school in the mornings and be with him in the evenings. The club also helped me in every way that they could.

But when Randall had a sensory overload, I was, unfortunately, the only one that could help him. And sensory overloads happened a lot more than I liked. It made me feel as if I was failing him as a parent, though I continued to remind myself that I still had a lot to learn about his needs.

Genesis grabbed my arm, dragging me to a stop before I could follow Randall inside. "I need to get inside to him," I told her, knowing how Randall could get if *anything* was out of whack.

She surprised me by wrapping her arms around my neck and slanting her lips across mine in a short, brief kiss, but it still made my blood pump faster through my veins. "That's my thank you," she breathed.

I reached up to rub the pad of my thumb over her bottom lip, watching as it trembled beneath my touch and her cheeks flushed.

"Maybe one day, I can properly thank you for introducing that amazing kid into my life," I huskily spoke. Cupping the back of her neck, I pressed a kiss to her forehead because if I kissed her fucking lips again, I wasn't sure if I'd be able to stop. "But for now, it has to wait."

With that, I released her and walked into the clubhouse, trying to think of anything but the way her curves had felt pressed against me.

I was so fucked.

Penny bumped my hip with hers as she stood next to where I was seated at the bar, watching Genesis help

Randall with his homework. Somehow, the way she explained it clicked in his brain.

Probably why she was a teacher.

"That's a damn good woman right there. Bit of a temper, but she'll keep you on your toes," Penny commented.

I grunted, taking a swallow of my beer. Genesis had been giving me hell all damn evening "She's a fucking stubborn one."

Penny laughed. "The best normally are."

I frowned at her. "You never really gave Copper the kind of hell Genesis is giving me," I remembered. Nah, instead, Penny had been all too willing to please Copper. She doted on him just as much as he doted on her.

Penny got a sad look in her eyes. I instantly internally kicked myself. "Things were a lot different for me," she said softly. She covered my hand with hers, and I hated that it trembled. "I was desperate for a hero, Halen. I couldn't save myself." She nodded her head in Genesis's direction. "But that woman right there? She doesn't need a hero. She's strong as fuck. She just needs a stabilizer; that's all."

I pressed a kiss to her cheek. "Get that sad look out of your eyes, woman," I told her. She laughed, but it sounded sad. "Or I'll go get Copper."

"What about me?" my president rumbled as he came up behind Penny and wrapped his arms around her waist.

Her eyes brightened in a way only he had ever been capable of making her light up.

"I was just talking to Halen," she told him. "I was just remembering how we met."

He brushed his nose along the column of her throat. She moaned. I stood up, laughing. "And that's my cue." I raised my beer to them. "Have fun. Make sure someone is watching the kids."

Copper flipped me the finger. I snorted and walked over to Genesis and Randall. "How's he doing?" I asked her.

"He just finished," she told me as Randall began to put his homework into his folder and pack his bag up.

"Want to come to my place for dinner?" I asked her.

Her cheeks flushed, and I had a feeling she was thinking about my earlier promise of properly thanking her. I grinned. "Just food, babe," I assured her. "I have no other intentions tonight." She rolled her eyes at me. "*But* if something happens to happen, well, it just happens."

She laughed and looked over at Randall. "Is he always so cocky and sure of himself?" she asked him.

Randall nodded. "He's the coolest."

Genesis rolled her eyes and stood, obviously internally disagreeing with Randall. "Yes, I'll take you up on that offer of dinner."

I grinned at her. "Thought you might. Come on, kiddo. Let's go home."

Randall immediately shouldered his bag and placed his hand in mine, letting me lead him out to my truck.

CHAPTER FOUR
HALEN

Dinner went off without a hitch, and Randall even went to bed without a fight, probably all tuckered out from his afternoon and evening spent with Genesis. Django curled up on his bed with him as was their normal routine, and I made sure Randall was deep asleep before I offered to take Genesis on a walk around the property.

It was a perfect night out. The temperature was just right, and the sky was clear, the moon shining brightly.

"You up for a walk?" I asked Genesis, pulling her eyes away from a picture of all of us club guys. I had just been patched in, and we were having a celebratory party.

I had finally found somewhere I belonged.

"You guys are like a family, aren't you?" she asked me.

I nodded, opening the front door for her. She stepped outside, and I quickly stepped out behind her, quietly shutting the front door behind me. "Besides my brother, the Savage Crows are all I've got, and no matter what, we stick together. Doesn't matter what kind of bullshit gets thrown our way."

She smiled. "It's envious."

I tossed her a smirk as we walked down the steps onto my gravel drive. "All you have to do is agree to be my old lady, and you'll be part of the family, too," I winked, laying it on thick.

She shot me a deadpan look that only made me laugh, not deterring me in the slightest. I was determined to claim this woman as mine, and I wasn't stopping until I accomplished it.

"So, tell me about Randall," she requested.

I stuffed my hands in my jeans pockets to keep from reaching out and touching her. This woman was like a fucking magnet.

"Randall has Autism and also suffers from ADHD," I told her. She gaped at me. "He's low on the spectrum, but there are still little things that set him off, like his schedule being out of whack, loud noises - little things like that. Or if he gets overwhelmed by anything, he tends to have meltdowns, but I'm getting better at keeping him from reaching those points."

Her eyes softened toward me. "I have him go to therapy twice a week. Sometimes, he does good, and he talks to his therapist about what he went through with his dad, and other times, he just sits silently the entire time. It depends on the day and his mood." I shrugged. "But I'm always patient with him, as are all of the other guys in the club." I swallowed thickly, more emotion than I'd ever thought I'd been capable of having towards a child closing up my throat. "I love that kid. I'm doing the best that I fucking can with him."

Genesis grabbed my hand in hers, linking our fingers together. My heart skirted all over my chest. "You're doing incredible with him, Halen," she assured me. God, she had no idea how much those words meant to me. "That little boy that I just spent my evening with? He's happy. I've never seen him so happy and talkative. He was even open about homework help and asking me questions about things he didn't understand. It's only been what – a month? And you're already making so much progress with him."

I stopped and turned toward her. Reaching up, I cupped her jaw, rubbing my thumb over her cheek. "I'll admit, some days with him, I feel like ripping my fucking hair out." She laughed, and somehow, I knew she completely understood. "But even though Randall isn't my blood, he's *my* kid; he's always going to be my kid, Genesis. You don't ever have to worry about him." Tears flooded her eyes. "As long as I have him, he's always going to be safe and taken care of," I promised her.

Surprising the fuck out of me, she leaned up on her tiptoes and wound her arms around my neck, angling her head to kiss me. With a soft, primal growl, I gripped her ass in my hands, yanking her closer to me, my mouth devouring hers as I quickly forced her into submission, leading her now instead of the other way around.

She moaned, not seeming to mind at all. This woman was a fucking vixen.

"Goddammit, woman," I growled, my lips running over her jaw. The sexiest fucking sound crawled up her throat as her hands slid under my shirt, gliding over my abs. They quivered beneath her touch.

Fuck, I needed her beneath me screaming my fucking name – and soon.

"Truck," I growled. I leaned back to look at her. I would never force her. I needed her fucking consent because I knew how much she had been against sex with me. "Please, for the love of God, tell me you fucking want this."

She nodded, her hand sliding into mine again as she led me towards my truck. I didn't even bother getting into the backseat. I just dropped the tailgate and lifted her up so she was sitting on the edge.

I yanked her thighs apart and laced my fingers in her hair, yanking her lips back down to mine as I pressed my hand to her lower back, yanking her body so close to mine that I couldn't tell where hers ended and mine began.

Her hands pushed at my cut, and with a grunt, I took it off, tossing it into the back of my truck before I pulled my lips from hers and pulled my shirt over my head, tossing it into the back as well. A pleased sigh fell from her lips as she ran her hands over me.

I groaned, my hands gripping her thighs. I seriously wondered if this woman had ever been touched by a fucking man before because the way she was looking at me? There was no fucking way.

I pulled her shirt over her head, her bra following next. I grabbed her breasts in my hands, pulling and tweaking her nipples as I kissed her again, swallowing all of her needy little sounds as they spilled from her lips.

She had no fucking idea how hard my cock was for her, and it was taking everything in me not to say fuck foreplay and bury myself in her to the fucking hilt - to fuck her until it goddamn hurt.

I undid her jeans and yanked them down her legs with her panties as she kicked her flats off, leaving her completely naked in front of me. Shooting her a wicked smirk, I dropped to my knees on the ground in front of her.

"Halen, I don't— Oh, *fuuuck*," she cried out, her fingers sliding into my hair, pulling on the strands.

I growled against her pussy, shoving her legs further apart. She fell back on the tailgate as I sucked at her clit, almost making her come for me, but I stopped just in time.

"What—why?" she protested, making me grin.

"Because the first time I make you cum, babe, you're going to cum all over my fucking cock," I promised as I hopped into the back of the truck with her.

I didn't even come out of my jeans. I just unsnapped my jeans and pulled my cock out, snatching a condom from my wallet. After sheathing myself, I knelt between her legs.

"Halen, wait," she breathlessly spoke right before I slid inside of her.

My arms shook as I let my eyes meet hers. If she told me to stop, I would. It would be hard as fuck, but I would stop.

"What?" I rumbled, breathing hard as I waited on her to tell me what the fuck was the problem.

"I'm a virgin," she blurted, her voice trembling, her eyes giving away her fucking nervousness.

Like *hell* was I *ever* fucking letting her walk away from me after that goddamn confession.

"If you don't have a fucking problem with me taking that card from you, then I don't give a damn," I retorted. She relaxed beneath me again. I leaned down, forcing myself to go slow, letting my lips meet hers. "I'm going to make this as painless as possible, but it's going to hurt," I warned her.

She nodded. "I trust you."

God, those words were going to be my undoing.

I lined my cock up with her slit and slowly eased inside of her. Taking her lips in a hard bruising kiss, I waited until she was completely lost in my lips before I shoved the rest of the way in, quickly ripping past her barrier.

She squeaked in shock, her nails digging into my shoulders. Her breath shuddered out of her as pain raced through my shoulder blades. "That hurt less than I expected," she finally uttered.

"Like ripping a fucking Band-Aid off," I grumbled.

She laughed, and the sound was like music to my fucking ears. I wanted to hear her laugh for the rest of my damn life.

Pressing a more tender kiss to her lips, I reached between us and rubbed my thumb over her clit. She mewled, her legs falling even further apart. "You good?"

"Better than good," she breathed.

I slowly began to move, allowing her body to adjust more to my size before I finally began to take her the way I wanted.

Savagely. Almost out of control.

And the sounds she made as she linked her ankles behind my back, meeting me thrust for thrust? She fucking loved it.

"Halen—" she whimpered.

I reached between us and rubbed her clit. She cried out my name as her pussy clenched my cock so tightly that I stopped breathing for a moment, her own orgasm triggering my own. I growled into her neck, my hands fisting on the bed of the truck as I tried not to lose my fucking mind.

I dropped to the side of her, my chest heaving up and down, sweat glistening on my skin. "Holy shit," I finally breathed.

"Is it always like that?" she gasped.

I wanted to laugh, but breathing was already enough of a struggle as it was. "Fuck no," I told her. "That was fucking *mind-blowing*."

She laughed a little, a yawn falling from her lips afterward. Without a word, I reached over and pulled her against my side, winding both of my arms around her. "Get some rest," I told her. "I'll take you inside in a little bit. Right now, I don't think I'm capable of fucking moving."

She nodded in agreement, her head resting on my shoulder as she yawned again, quickly passing out right after. I glanced up at the sky as my breathing slowly returned to normal, my heart rate decreasing with it.

God help me because I wanted this woman as mine. Would I fuck up along the way? Guaran-fucking-tee it. But would it deter me at all? Fuck no.

Genesis was going to be *mine*.

CHAPTER FIVE
HALEN

Waking up by myself in the back of my truck with a stiff back was not the way I had planned to start my morning.

There was no sign of Genesis around my place. She was gone – as if she hadn't even been there in the first place.

And it put me in a sour as fuck mood.

The woman had even disposed of my fucking condom. It was almost as if she had wanted to pretend the night had ever happened, so she had gotten rid of every bit of evidence.

I sat up and stretched my arms over my head, scowling at the still mostly-dark sky. Clouds were now covering the once empty, starlit sky. Today would be a gloomy day – a perfect match for my foul as fuck mood.

If Genesis thought she was getting rid of me that fucking easily, she had another thing coming for her. I wasn't that kind of man. I didn't stop until I had what I wanted.

And I wanted Genesis as my old lady.

Buttoning my jeans, I jumped out of the back of my truck and grabbed all my clothes, storming up to the house. It wasn't time for Randall to be up yet to get ready for school, so I had time to shower and get dressed and get at least two cups of coffee in my system.

And maybe a couple of ibuprofen, too. My damn back was aching like a mother fucker. I was too old for fucking in the back of my truck anymore.

After taking a quick shower, I yanked on a pair of jeans and a t-shirt, shrugging my cut on after. Once I was downstairs, I began brewing a pot of coffee, grunting in annoyance when my phone rang on the counter.

"What, Copper?" I grumbled.

"You're in a pissy mood," he noted.

"It's four-something in the fucking morning, and I haven't had a bit of caffeine to help me deal with your ass," I retorted. He barked out a laugh. I swear, these days I felt like Copper lived to annoy the shit out of me. "What do you want?"

"Need you to go into the shop early. Kyle is going to be running late. Skylar isn't feeling well," I rolled my eyes. His wife was a pain in the ass when she was sick. She hated being doted on and taken care of. Kyle was going to have a hell of a day. "I told Kyle I would find someone to open the shop. Penny can take Randall to school."

I glanced toward the stairs. "I don't know, Copper. You know how Randall is about his routine being messed with," I reminded him. "There's no way of knowing if it might set him off."

"Penny will follow every step you take when you take him to school in the mornings," Copper assured me, understanding in his tone. "Besides, Randall adores Penny," he reminded me. "Don't worry. It won't be bad. He'll do fine."

"Everyone adores Penny," I reminded Copper.

I could practically picture his smirk. "I know. My wife is fucking amazing."

I rolled my eyes. Copper was a cocky son of a bitch, especially when it came to Penny.

Sighing, I began making myself a cup of coffee, not even giving the pot time to finish filling up. The warming eye on the coffee machine sizzled and hissed as coffee dripped onto it while I poured some into a large mug.

"He'll be at the garage with me," I told Copper. "And tell her not to worry about breakfast. I'll feed him before I leave here. Randall doesn't like eating in a car, and he doesn't eat at school with the other kids."

"Got it," Copper said. "We owe you one."

"Nah," I grunted. "Don't owe me shit. I'm hanging up now. I need caffeine."

I hung up the phone, not giving Copper a chance to say anything else. He and I gave each other shit all of the time. Copper was the closest I had to both a parental figure and a blood brother. I hated it when he told me he owed me for doing something like this.

I owed Copper my entire fucking life for saving mine. I would be paying that debt to him until my last, dying breath.

I watched as Genesis stepped into the office, looking as tired as I felt. I didn't even feel bad that she hadn't gotten a good night's rest. If she had stayed like I wanted her to, I could have carried her inside of the house and put her to bed, went for round two, and we could have passed out together until I had to get Randall up for school.

She was the one that took off in the middle of the night – not me.

Penny stepped into the garage, smiling at me. I instantly smiled back at her. She handed me a steaming cup of coffee from Rosanna's. "Is he doing okay?" she asked me, referring to Randall.

I glanced over to where he was reading a kid's book on my phone. I nodded. "He asked to read when I got here." I shrugged. "He's been quiet since I gave him my phone. So far, so good."

"Thank you again for opening the shop this morning," she told me. "Kyle will be in soon."

I pressed a kiss to each of her cheeks. "Thanks for being such a great auntie to him," I told her, referring to Randall. "He loves you."

A throat cleared to the side of us, and both of us looked over to see Genesis standing there. Her face was red, and she was furious. I resisted the urge to smirk.

She might have taken off from me last night, but the woman had a fucking jealous streak in her.

I loved it.

"Did you know your boyfriend was with me last night?" she snapped at Penny.

Penny rolled her lips into her mouth to keep from laughing, her eyes catching Copper's as he strode into the garage with Kyle behind him. Kyle looked like shit, but he had a cup of coffee in his hands and looked to be slowly waking up.

But me? I burst into laughter, unable to help myself. This woman was my soulmate. There was no doubt in my fucking mind about that.

"What's so damn funny?" Kyle asked as Copper walked up and wound his arms around Penny's waist, pressing a kiss to her lips.

Genesis instantly turned an embarrassing shade of red, her mouth opening and closing like a fish. "I - I, oh, my God. I'm so sorry," she rushed out, apologizing to Penny. "I didn't - I thought—"

Penny laughed. "It's okay, hun. No harm done." She held her hand out to Genesis. "My name is Penny." Genesis quickly shook her hand, her cheeks still flaming red. I leaned against the car behind me, still highly amused. "This is my husband, Copper. He's the president of the MC."

"I'm still so sorry—" Genesis quickly apologized, but Penny cut her off.

"No need to apologize, Genesis. The men are just incredibly sweet and protective of me; that's all," she assured her. "Copper would kill them if they made a serious move on me."

I laughed. That much was fucking true. Copper was the most territorial man out of all of us.

"I'm just going to go, um, work," Genesis stammered, quickly turning on her heel to flee into the office.

"Hey, Genesis," I called. Her back stiffened, and she glared at me over her shoulder. I smirked. "Maybe if you hadn't run the fuck off in the middle of the night, you would have known that I'm actually a hundred percent available to you."

Her fists clenched at her sides. Without saying anything to me, she stormed into the office, slamming the door shut behind her. I drew in a deep breath, shaking my head.

That woman was going to work my last nerve.

"Give it time, brother," Kyle told me as he ruffled Randall's hair. Randall's eyes never moved from my phone screen. "She's clearly into you."

"Then what's the fucking deal?" I snapped, now agitated once again. "Why can't she be fucking simple and not fight me every step of the damn way?"

Kyle laughed. "First things first, brother, don't ever try calling a woman out on their shit." I scowled at him. "They'll shut you down faster than you can ever fucking apologize."

I growled and turned away from him, walking over to Randall. "Hey, kid. You ready to go to school?"

He looked up at me. "Can I finish reading this when I get out of school?" he asked.

"After you finish your homework," I told him. I knelt in front of him and took my phone, locking it and shoving it into my pocket. "Are you going to be okay if I don't take you?" I asked him.

He nodded. "I'm a big boy, Dad. I can handle it."

I smiled at him. *God, I loved this kid.* "If you need me, tell Auntie Penny to call me, understand?" He nodded. "Words, Randall," I reminded him.

"Yes, sir."

I smiled at him. This kid had me wrapped around his fucking finger. "Good. Go to Auntie Penny, okay? She's going to walk you to your class just like I do every morning."

He got down from his chair and wrapped his arms around my neck, pressing a kiss to my cheek. My heart constricted in my chest. "I love you, Dad."

"I love you, too, kid," I said roughly, squeezing him to me just a little. "Be good, okay?"

He nodded and grabbed his backpack, walking over to Penny. She shot me a smile as she grabbed his hand and began leading him out to her SUV.

"Does that shit ever become less emotional?" I asked as Damon stepped into the garage.

"Nope," Damon answered as Copper also shook his head at me. "Fucks with you every damn time," he warned me. "So, do your best to get used to it."

With that, he walked over to the toolbox and grabbed what he needed to start working. I shook my head.

Damon had gotten the love of his life back, including his daughter, and Cassidy was currently pregnant with their second baby.

Around his family, he was a hell of a lot softer. Around the rest of us? He was still a dick. But he wouldn't be Damon if he wasn't.

Shaking my head, I began to work, deciding to ignore Genesis's presence for the rest of the day. That woman was going to be a piece of work, and I needed time to get my head on straight before I continued to pursue her. Because if I didn't, I knew I was just going to fuck up more.

And I couldn't afford to do that. I wanted her to be mine.

CHAPTER SIX
GENESIS

I hadn't expected Olivia to show up, but she stepped into the office about thirty minutes after Halen's snide remark to me. "I'm here to train you," she told me. "Kyle told me he hired you and just stuck you in the office." She rolled her eyes. "That man is something else, I swear."

I couldn't help but smile. Instantly, she was likable. "I'm sure you know who I am," she continued, "but I'll introduce myself anyway. I'm Olivia, Brett's wife."

"I saw you at the clubhouse yesterday," I told her, reaching forward to shake her hand.

She shot me a knowing smile. "Seems that you've caught Halen's attention," she noted.

I frowned. "Why is he so persistent?" I asked her. "It's a bit alarming. He won't take no for an answer."

"These men know what they want, and they go after it," she told me. "And Halen wants you. It's as plain and simple as that."

I made a disgruntled sound. "But I'm sure there are any number of women that want him. Why can't he go bother them?"

"He *could*," she said with a shrug. Jealousy ripped through me, just as it had earlier when I saw him kiss Penny's cheek. "But he doesn't want them. He wants you."

"We slept together last night," I blurted. My cheeks flamed red. *Did I seriously have no filter between my brain and my mouth anymore?*

Olivia had the audacity to laugh. I scowled at her. "Oh, you've done it now, girl. You really think Halen is going to get one night out of you and call it quits?" she asked me. I frowned. "I'll give you a little piece of advice. It's up to you what you do with it," she told me. I looked up at her. "Don't fight him on this. It's clear as hell that you want him, too. By fighting him, you're setting both of you up for misery, and honestly, I don't want to see either of you all twisted up. Just give him a chance."

I shook my head. "No. He's a dick," I snapped.

Olivia shrugged. "Sure, they all are," she agreed. I almost laughed. "But you haven't seen the way they are when they're with the one they love." On cue, Brett stepped into the office, and instantly, his scowl left his face as his eyes landed on Olivia. She squeaked in shock when he yanked her to him and pressed his lips to hers.

"Hey, babe," he greeted her, handing her a cup of coffee and a small, brown bag. "Got your favorite since I knew you were aggravated at Kyle this morning."

She beamed at him and leaned up to press another kiss to his lips. "You're the best," she told him, making him grin at her.

He pressed a kiss to her forehead. "I'll be at the other garage today. Try not to kill Kyle, will you?"

She laughed. "This should do the trick," she assured him, holding up the coffee and brown bag. "I love you. Be careful."

"Always, babe."

He walked out of the office, shutting the door back behind him. She took a sip of the coffee, releasing a pleased sigh. "See? This is what you're missing out on," she told me.

I shook my head. I didn't feel like I was missing out on anything except great sex . . . and maybe seeing Halen as a dad. God, seeing him with Randall made me crave him. He was so gentle and warm with him. It was such a change from how he was with me and everyone else.

"Spill it," Olivia demanded, making me jerk my eyes back to her. "Something is bothering you, and it's not just Halen."

I frowned. She was right. It wasn't just Halen. Honestly, I would have loved to stay all night with him, but I had bigger things to worry about.

Turns out, those bigger things had done me a favor anyway. It revealed how dickish Halen could be. Who the fuck blurted that kind of shit in front of other people?

"I left Halen in the middle of the night," I told her. She frowned at me. "But not for the reason he seems to think." I dropped into a chair. I felt like the weight of the world was on my shoulders. "I'm getting threatened with eviction. I had to go home and make sure I didn't get locked out of my apartment." Understanding dawned on Olivia's face. Tears burned in my eyes. I was so exhausted and worn down these days, and talking about it helped as much as it made it all the more real. "I'm hoping that I can at least give my landlord my first check from here in the hopes that he'll let me stay as I continue to catch up."

"Oh, sweetheart," Olivia whispered. "How long has this been going on?"

"A month now," I told her. "I was a teacher – specifically Randall's teacher. And I lost my job for helping him, and they told everyone I was inappropriate with a student. It's cut me off from all other teaching positions."

Tears spilled down my cheeks. Olivia instantly wrapped her arms around me. "Hun, all you have to do is say something to Kyle. He'll give you an advance."

I shook my head. I couldn't ask that of him. He was already doing so much by giving me a job off the word of Halen and paying me so damn well. I would get myself out of this bind with time.

I swiped at my cheeks. "I'm sorry that I'm such a mess," I croaked. "I haven't been able to talk to anyone about this. All of my old friends cut me off as soon as news of why I lost my teaching position spread."

"They're fucking idiots," Olivia retorted. I laughed, though it sounded broken. She handed me a tissue. "Dry your eyes and tilt your chin up," she ordered. "You're strong. You'll figure this out."

I smiled at her. "Thanks, Olivia."

She beamed at me. It was easy to see why Brett was so infatuated with her. "Anytime, Genesis. We're a family here," she said, squeezing my hand. "And us women have to stick together."

And suddenly, even though I wasn't with Halen, I felt like she had already welcomed me in.

Honestly, it felt really damn good.

I'd avoided Halen all day, and when he had come into the office to order a part, he hadn't said a word to me. He had just walked over to the other computer in the room, ordered what he needed, and walked out again, not even casting me a glance.

I knew I had continuously shut him down and running off without a word had probably been the worst thing to do, but his actions kind of cut deep.

I'd been expecting him to still chase me, and I hadn't realized I wanted that from him until he was no longer paying me any attention.

When the end of the day came, he still hadn't said a word to me. In fact, when I was closing up the office, he wasn't even at the shop anymore.

With a tired, exhausted sigh, I unlocked the door to my apartment, my shoulders relaxing in relief when I realized the locks hadn't been changed. I hadn't been evicted - *yet*.

The key word was yet. I had a gut feeling that it would be coming soon, though.

I flicked the light switch for the kitchen, frowning when it didn't come on. Thinking a bulb must have blown, I tried a different one, groaning when it didn't come on either.

I twisted the knob to turn the water on in the kitchen sink. Nope. Not a damn drop.

"Fuck," I sighed. I dropped my face into my hands, trying not to cry. I hadn't been evicted yet, which was a plus, but now I had no electricity and no water.

And even worse, no money.

My life was turning to shit, and it was happening a hell of a lot faster than I was capable of coping with.

CHAPTER SEVEN
HALEN

I frowned as I leaned against Genesis's open doorway, watching as she flicked her light switch on, trying another one and then the faucet before she realized her water and her electricity had been turned off.

But if I knew one thing about Genesis so far, it was that she was stubborn as all hell. She wouldn't come to anyone for help.

Olivia had come to me around lunchtime, informing me of what was going on with Genesis, expressing her concern, but I told Olivia to stay out of it. If there was one thing I knew about Genesis, it was that she would take a handout of money as someone treating her like a charity case.

And I was already walking on thin ice with her as it was.

But thankfully, Drake and I had grown up with the water and electricity at home being turned off so often that we had eventually learned to watch the city guy when he came out so we knew how to turn it all back on again.

"You need some help?" I asked when she leaned down against her kitchen counter and buried her face in her hands. I hated seeing her like this – so worn down by the shit hand that life had dealt her, especially when she had done nothing wrong.

All she had tried to do was help a little boy.

She spun around to face me so fast that she stumbled, but she caught herself on the counter before she fell on her ass. I stuffed my hands in the pockets of my jeans. "I can help you get your water and electric back on," I told her.

Immediately, a scowl twisted her beautiful features. I heaved a heavy sigh, honestly tired of this back and forth shit with her all of the time.

Why did I have to want the one woman in the world who didn't seem to want a damn thing to do with me?

"Olivia told you, didn't she?" she seethed. I just stayed silent. I wouldn't rat Olivia out like that. She had honestly been concerned, and it had taken a lot of talking down with Brett's help to get her to keep her nose out of everything. "I want you to leave, Halen, and I want you to leave me the fuck alone, you hear me? I'm not a fucking charity case, and I don't like being treated like one." She gritted her teeth. "Go!" she snapped at me.

My fingers twitched with the urge to wrap my hand around her throat, shove her against the wall, and remind her of who the fuck she was talking to, but I reined my temper in.

This woman was a fucking work of art.

Shaking my head, I spun on my heel and marched down the stairs from her small apartment, going over to my bike. After grabbing the tool I needed, I walked over to her electric and water meter, and after fiddling around for a minute, I heard the telltale sign of her water running in her kitchen sink, and I watched the lights in her kitchen flicker on.

Genesis rushed to the window and flung it open, her wide, beautiful eyes staring down at me in shock and incredulity. I just smirked at her and walked back over to my bike, throwing a wave over my shoulder.

I had her. Something in my gut told me that after that, she'd be eating most of the words she'd thrown my way since meeting me.

"We're having a cookout over at the clubhouse in a little bit," I called as I straddled my bike, strapping my helmet to my head. "You should come out and get something to eat."

With that, I revved my engine and spun out of the gravel lot, heading down the highway to the clubhouse.

"Kid, over here!" I shouted at Randall. He'd wanted to play a game of football, and so, all of us men plus Ryker were running around the back of the clubhouse where it was grassy, playing shirts against skins.

Damon tackled me down, preventing me from catching the ball when Randall threw it to me. "Fuck," I wheezed, the breath knocked from my body.

Damon stood and held his hand out to me, helping me up as well. "Not as young as we used to be, huh?" he commented, shaking his head as he laughed. "I think tackling you hurt me as much as it hurt you to hit the ground like that."

I looked up when a familiar Toyota pulled into the lot. Genesis slid out a moment later, and Randall immediately took off toward her, a shit-eating grin on his face. Vincent strolled up beside me, letting loose a low whistle. I jabbed my elbow into his ribs.

"You hitting that?" he teasingly asked me.

"Yeah. Keep your fucking hands and eyes off," I ordered. He cast me a grin. "She's just being stubborn as fuck," I told him.

He laughed. "The best ones normally are," he reminded me. "How long are you planning on chasing her?"

"As long as it takes," I told him honestly. "She's it."

He moved away as Genesis walked over to me with Randall's hand in her own. I knelt down in front of Randall. "Hey, kiddo, you mind going to get my shirt and my cut?" I asked him.

He nodded, his eyes lighting up at the mention of my cut. He loved being able to hold it. It made him feel invincible or some shit – like he had a coat of armor on.

I stood up. "Sorry about being shirtless," I apologized to Genesis. Her cheeks were flaming red, and she was having a hard as hell time looking away from my tattooed chest and abs. "Randall wanted to play football, so we played shirts against skins," I explained.

"Doesn't that hurt?" she asked me.

"Nah." I ruffled Randall's hair as he handed me my shirt. I tugged it on over my head, shrugging my cut on afterward. "Go play, kid." He dashed off, going to find Ryker. I looked back at Genesis. "Not much hurts worse than two bullet wounds in your back." I shrugged.

Her face paled. "You've been shot?"

I snorted. "All of us men here have," I told her honestly. "It's our life."

She was fiddling with her fingers, doing a little dance in place like she was extremely nervous.

"I'm sorry," she finally blurted. I arched an eyebrow at her, not expecting her to have apologized for anything. "I was such a bitch for no reason. Besides being a bit crude, you've been kind, and I had no reason to lash out at you like I've been doing, and—"

I grabbed her face in my hands and leaned down, silencing her with a hard kiss that had my cock hardening in my jeans. She moaned low in her throat, her hands coming up to grip my sides.

"Shut up," I grumbled against her lips. "I don't want your apologies. If you want to apologize, then stay here, eat some damn good food, and spend time with me and Randall," I told her.

"That easy?" she whispered, her eyes roaming my face.

I nodded at her. "That fucking easy, babe." I brushed my thumb over her bottom lip. "One day, when I finally get you to agree to be mine," she shot me a deadpan look that made me smirk, "you'll realize that everything with me is fucking easy."

She rolled her eyes. "I doubt that considering you're constantly wearing on my nerves."

I smirked and planted another kiss on her lips, this one a bit softer than the last one had been. "Just enjoy the evening with me," I pleaded with her. "No strings attached; I promise." I blew out a harsh breath. My next words were going to kill me, but this was the kind of woman who liked having control of her life and her decisions. "I'll back off."

A small frown pulled at her lips, like she didn't like what I had said. That time, it was my turn to frown in confusion. What the hell was going on in her damn head?

"And if I don't want you to back off?" she bravely asked me.

Something stirred in my chest – hope, maybe? "Then I won't," I told her. "I'll fucking claim you, babe. You'll be mine."

She placed her hands on my chest. I thought she might push me away, but she just rested them there. "We'll see," she finally murmured.

Best fucking words I'd heard yet.

CHAPTER EIGHT
GENESIS

I watched Halen as he covered Randall up with a blanket, making sure he was securely wrapped in it. Somehow, I knew I would never grow tired of watching him take care of Randall. Halen was an amazing dad, and there was never any annoyance on his face when he dealt with his son.

Like earlier, when Randall had a small meltdown because his ketchup wasn't spread completely over his bun. Halen had taken him back over to the table where the food was laid out, and together, they made a new burger with Randall supervising, calming the little boy instantly. Most parents would have just told Randall to shut up and eat it, but Halen calmly dealt with the situation.

After he was sure Randall was completely settled in, Halen walked over to me. "Sorry that took a bit of time. Normally, he sleeps with Django, but when we're at the clubhouse, he normally sleeps with me. I don't want to disturb him, though. It normally sets him off." I nodded in understanding. "So, I have to make sure he feels secure while he's sleeping."

I frowned. I hated that his father had messed with him so much. No child deserved to feel like they weren't completely safe and loved, but I knew given enough time, Halen would resurrect every wrong done to Randall.

Halen reached up and tucked my hair behind my ear. The move was such an intimate one from him that my heart constricted in my chest. All evening, he had been showing me he was capable of tenderness, and it was fucking with my soul.

"You going home, or do you want to stay here with me?" he asked.

Drawing in a deep breath, I decided to take a step. I was insanely attracted to him, not to mention the fact that while he did get on my nerves a lot, he had a way about him that just *spoke* to me.

"I'll stay," I told him quietly.

Grabbing my hand in his, he linked our fingers together and led me up a small flight of stairs and down a hall. He unlocked a door and stepped in, shutting it behind us. "This is basically where I used to live until I took in Randall," Halen explained as he flicked on a lamp. "I had the place that I took you out to, but I preferred to be here. I've got some clothes here for me and Randall, but that's basically it. You should be able to find something to sleep in over there." He pointed to a dresser. "I need a fucking shower. I smell like ass."

I barked out a laugh. I couldn't help it. He'd said it with the most serious expression on his face. Halen had a fucking sense of humor about him that was contagious.

Shaking his head at me, he pressed a short kiss to my lips and walked into the bathroom, shutting the door behind him. His little kisses were becoming frustrating. I knew he was trying to leave the cards in my hands, but I wanted him to take the lead on this. I had no idea what I was doing.

I mean, fuck; he'd been the one to take my damn virginity, for fuck's sake.

Drawing in a deep breath, I stripped out of my clothes and waited until I heard the telltale signs of him being in the shower before I quietly slipped into the bathroom. The mirror was already fogging, steam already filling the small room.

And fuck, his body under the water had my nipples so hard they hurt. My belly clenched, and wetness pooled between my thighs. How was one man so damn sinfully hot?

I stepped into the shower, and the rustling of the clear shower curtain had him turning to face me. I swallowed thickly as I watched the water run down his tattooed chest, sliding down the valley of his abs. I didn't dare look further – wasn't sure if I could control myself if I did.

"Woman," Halen growled. A single word, and yet, it held all of the warning I needed.

I knew if I stayed in this shower with him, Halen would take me like a man starved, and God, I *wanted* him to.

"Halen," I whispered, "please."

His eyes darkened, and he stepped closer to me, reaching up to cup the side of my neck, using his thumb to tilt my head back. "You sure this is what you want?"

"Yes," I whispered, my eyes locked with his.

He narrowed his eyes at me. "If you take off in the middle of the night again, I won't give a fuck who's around us the next time I see you. I will bend you over and spank your pretty little ass red," he warned me.

Oh, God. I was pretty sure I moaned at his words.

His lips met mine in a hard, bruising kiss, and he quickly coaxed my lips apart, his tongue tangling with mine. Every bit of him assaulted my senses. I couldn't think of anything else *but* him.

Halen consumed me.

Backing me up against the shower wall, he bent his head, taking a hard nipple between his teeth, gently biting before he flicked his tongue over it, soothing it before sucking it hard. I cried out, my hands clawing at his shoulders.

His calloused hand slid between my thighs, and I quickly parted my legs, giving him better access. I whimpered as the heel of his hand brushed my clit, my nails digging into his shoulders in response.

"God, you're so fucking *wet*," Halen growled. He moved over to my other breast, showering it with the same attention as he slid a finger inside of me. "So fucking *tight*."

"Halen," I whimpered, begging him for something, but unsure what. I could hardly think, and he had *just* begun touching me. I could barely stand it, and yet, I never wanted him to stop.

"I love it when you say my name," he rumbled. He stood up to his full height, his finger slowly sliding in and out of me, the heel of his hand still rubbing over my clit. My breath was shuddering in and out of me. I was panting. It felt so fucking good – too damn good to be true.

"Yes, baby." He took my lips in a hard kiss as I came hard, his tongue diving between my lips, swallowing my scream as I came hard around his finger.

My eyes slowly opened, my chest heaving up and down. He kissed me softer this time, and once my breathing regulated some, I wrapped my hand around his thick cock, watching as a shudder wracked his frame. He closed his eyes, his hands flattening on the wall on either side of my head.

"Fuck, baby," he rasped.

A little bit of pride rose in me – pride that I was capable of making him feel so much just by wrapping my hand around his cock. But I was still nervous.

I slowly dropped to my knees in front of him, looking up at him as I did so. His eyes were basically black as he stared down at me, his jaw clenched. "Will you show me?" I asked him.

"*Fuck*," he swore. I swallowed nervously. "Yeah, baby. I'll show you." He slid one of his hands into my hair. "Open your mouth."

I obediently did as he asked, and I moaned as he slipped his cock into my mouth, being careful not to go too deep as he slid the tip over my tongue. "Wrap your hand around the base of my cock," he guided. "The tip of my dick is the most sensitive spot for me," he informed me. "Since you're new at this, pay attention to the head. Use your hand to work the rest of me."

Doing as he said, I focused special attention to the tip of his cock, moaning when precum coated my tongue. He tightened his hold on my hair, thrusting lightly as I sucked, low moans crawling up his throat.

I was aching for him all over again.

"Touch yourself with your other hand," he roughly commanded.

I tentatively slid my hand between my legs, rubbing a circle over my clit. I moaned around the head of his cock. "Yes – fuck, yes, baby. I want to see you get yourself off," he told me.

I worked my fingers faster, occasionally slipping them inside of me before going back to my clit. When I finally came, Halen pulled back, and with two strokes, he came on my chest, his cum sliding all over my breasts.

"*Goddamn,*" he growled, staring at me with nothing but pure heat and something akin to adoration in his eyes. He pulled me up and yanked me against him, not even giving a shit about the cum on my chest. His lips took mine in a savage kiss before he lifted me up and slid deep inside of me, holding me up with sheer strength.

"Halen!" I cried out, my arms tangling around his neck. He pressed my back against the shower wall and fucked me hard and fast. It was almost painful, but I never wanted him to stop. I lost count of the number of times I came just from his pelvic bone repeatedly hitting my clit.

He quickly pulled out of me at the last second, coming on my stomach, kissing me again, this time slower and deeper. Our hearts were racing, both of us completely breathless.

"I'm never fucking letting you go," he rumbled in my ear as he continued holding me.

I buried my face in the crook of his neck, tightening my hold on him. "I never want you to," I whispered, finally admitting it to myself.

Despite everything, I was falling head over heels for this man, and I didn't even give the slightest fuck that he was a criminal.

Because to me and to Randall, he was one of the best men I had ever fucking known.

I jerked awake to the sound of a child screaming. Before I even had a chance to move a finger, Halen had already moved out from beneath me, yanking on a pair of sweats. He was already pounding down the stairs with a gun in his hand by the time I managed to get off of the bed.

I quickly pulled on a pair of his boxers and a t-shirt and rushed down the stairs after him. All of the adults that had stayed were awake and working on getting the other children back to sleep. Halen was sitting on the floor at the bottom of the staircase holding a sobbing Randall in his arms. His gun was laying forgotten beside him as he cradled the back of Randall's head, gently rocking him back and forth.

"Easy, son," Halen soothed. "It's okay. I won't let anyone hurt you, you know that." He leaned back some, looking down into Randall's pale, tear-stained face. "Who's the biggest monster, kiddo?"

Randall sniffled. "You," he croaked.

Halen pulled him back against his chest. "That's right. And I'll destroy *anyone* that dares to harm you. Don't ever forget that. You're *always* safe with me."

Tears burned in my eyes as I watched them together. I slowly bent down and picked up Halen's discarded weapon. He looked up at me, nodding once in acknowledgement before he stood up from the floor, still holding Randall as he ascended the stairs, whispering gentle, soothing words to his little boy.

Suddenly, I desperately wanted to be a part of their little family. I wanted it so badly that my chest ached.

I placed Halen's weapon back under his pillow, watching as he laid down on the bed, never letting Randall go. I covered them up before I got back in on the side I'd been on, but this time with Randall between us.

"Get closer," Halen told me, his tone booking no arguments. "He needs security."

He didn't ever have to tell me twice. I quickly got as close to Randall as I could, and Halen and I sandwiched him between us, both of our arms somehow managing to wrap around the little boy. I even went as far as to draw my knees up so I was completely wrapped around him.

It didn't take Randall long to fall back asleep. Halen met my eyes over Randall's head, and the pain in them tore at my soul. "I want to kill that son of a bitch," Halen growled.

I shook my head at him. "Let the law do its job," I whispered. "I know it's hard. I want the same damn thing as well, but we can't take this into our own hands."

Halen scoffed. "I fucking could, actually." I knew that - had no doubt about it, especially after he told me that every man in the club had been shot at least once. You didn't get bullet wounds by doing legal shit. He drew in a deep breath. "Thank you for being here."

"Always," I told him. His eyes locked on mine, an unspoken question in his gaze. I swallowed thickly. "I mean it, Halen." His eyes softened. "*Always.* I'm not going anywhere."

He closed his eyes, his body relaxing. "Always knew you were fucking amazing, babe."

He didn't mean it in a teasing way either. There was nothing but open, honest sincerity in his voice.

I swallowed past the sudden lump in my throat. I'd never had family, but right then, I knew I finally had one.

Somehow, I knew I would always belong with Halen.

I had no doubt in my mind that this man was it for me.

CHAPTER NINE
HALEN

I was sipping a scalding hot cup of coffee when Genesis strolled downstairs. Most of the guys were already up and gone for the day, heading in to work early. I watched as she looked around her in confusion, obviously looking for Randall. I'd let him keep his pajamas on and put him in the sitting area with a movie on my phone.

He was extremely out of sorts, and it was fucking with my head to see him like this. He hadn't even smiled when Penny made him his favorite breakfast of pancakes with whipped cream to help cheer him up. He had just played with his food, and for a kid that normally had such a big appetite, it was alarming as fuck.

"I'm taking Randall in to see his therapist today as soon as she opens," I informed Genesis. She frowned, concern swirling in her eyes for Randall. "He hasn't had a nightmare in a couple of weeks now. This one fucked with him pretty bad."

She placed her hand on my arm. "He'll be okay," she tried soothing me, but nothing would ease the anxiety twisting my gut.

I drew in a deep breath. "I fucking hope so. I hate seeing the kid like this. Fucking tears at me," I confessed.

About three that morning, Copper found me outside smoking a blunt, too wound up to continue lying in bed any longer. He'd silently sat beside me, being the support that I needed because I felt like my soul was ripping apart.

It felt like all of the progress Randall had been making was quickly dwindling. It left me spiraling.

Genesis suddenly wrapped her arms around my midsection, drawing me out of my head. I blew out a soft breath and folded my arms around her, burying my face in the crook of her neck, holding her tight against me. "Thanks for being here last night," I quietly told her. "It makes things a lot more bearable."

She pressed a kiss to my chest before she looked up at me with those pretty eyes. "I told you last night – always, Halen."

I reached up and rubbed the pad of my thumb over her bottom lip. "You're sure that you're ready for that, babe?"

She nodded. "I've never been surer of anything in my life," she told me honestly. "I want this with you; I want to be part of your family, Halen – even the club family."

I leaned down and took her lips in a soft, slow kiss. She moaned as I grabbed her ass, yanking her so close to me that it felt like our bodies were going to melt together.

Remembering that she had to go to work and I had a child to take care of, I released her with a groan, pressing a kiss to her forehead afterward. "Go on to work. I'll call you after his appointment, yeah?"

She nodded at me. "If you need me, call, Halen. I know enough about the club to know that Kyle will let me leave and come to you."

God, this woman was fucking incredible.

"Go on to work, babe," I told her again. "I'll call if I need you - promise," I assured her.

She nodded and walked over to Randall, leaning down to press a kiss to the top of his head. Surprising me, he got off of the couch and hugged her tightly, not letting go for at least a full minute. And that incredible woman of mine knelt down and folded her arms around him as well, holding him as long as he wanted to be held.

She was going to make a damn good mom.

Randall's therapist had suggested that Randall stay home from school for the rest of the week to allow his mind and his anxiety to settle. Apparently, bringing Genesis into his life had caused a disruption, and while Randall was extremely happy to have her as a part of his life, it still acted as a trigger.

She suggested that I keep him close to me to give him his sense of security back, so I was taking him to work. I had already called his school and told them that Randall would be staying home and that yes, he would have a damn school excuse.

And then I contacted my brother to inform him of what was going on so that when the damn school called him about Randall's absence, he would already be aware.

The last time something like this happened and his therapist suggested I keep him out of school for a couple of days, they had called my brother, informing him of Randall's absence.

It had pissed me off considering when there were *real* fucking complaints about him missing school, no one gave a damn and instead fired the teacher who was concerned for the student.

Shaking my head, I gritted my teeth, making the turn I needed to head down the road that would lead to the garage. Her being fired was beginning to piss me off more and more as I thought about it. It wasn't fucking right.

Shaking my head a little, I made a mental note to talk to Copper, to see what strings he and Damon might be capable of pulling to get Genesis her teaching position back.

I also needed to see what we could do about getting everyone who failed to take her complaints seriously fired. It would only be a matter of time before those same people ignored someone else's complaint, and that shit didn't settle right with me.

I pulled onto the gravel lot, parking my truck off to the side near the fence. "Dad?" Randall asked. I turned in my seat to face him, giving him my undivided attention. "Is Genesis here?"

"She's here, kid," I told him.

He played with the hem of his shirt. "Can I sit with her?" he asked me.

I nodded at him. "Of course," I assured him. I hopped out of the truck, pocketing my keys before I strode over to the other side, helping Randall down from the backseat. He instantly placed his hand in mine as soon as his feet were on the ground, and I led him straight to the office, avoiding the noise in the garage. Some days it was okay for him, but I was a bit worried all the noise might be a bit much for him today.

Genesis looked up at our entrance. She was buried under paperwork, but she was at ease, not stressed in the slightest. Just the sight of all of those papers fucking made my skin crawl. I *hated* paperwork.

Randall released my hand and walked over to Genesis, crawling into her lap. She smiled down at him and pressed a kiss to the top of his head before she looked up at me. "Everything okay?"

I just shrugged at her. "Later," I told her. She nodded in understanding. I pulled my phone out of my pocket, pulling up a movie app and handing it to Randall. "Are you going to be good for Genesis?"

Randall nodded at me. "I'll be good," he promised.

I looked at my watch. "I haven't fed him lunch yet, so around eleven-thirty, I'll order something and have it delivered for all of us. Sound good?"

Genesis nodded at me. "Whatever you order will be fine," she assured me.

I leaned down and pressed a soft kiss to her lips. "If you need me, just let me know. I'll come in a little bit and check on him."

She smiled down at Randall who was already engrossed in a kid's movie, not paying either of us any attention. "I'm sure we'll be fine, Halen. Go on to work. The guys are buried."

I rolled my eyes. "When aren't we?" I grumbled. With a heavy sigh, I pressed a kiss to the top of Randall's head and headed out to the garage to get to work.

But before I walked out of the door, I turned and looked over my shoulder at Genesis. Feeling my eyes on her, she looked back up, her cheeks warming under my intense gaze. "You're fucking amazing, babe," I told her honestly.

Her eyes brightened at my words. Flashing her a smile, I finally left the office. Copper looked up at me. "Everything good?"

I sighed. "Good as it's going to be right now," I told him honestly.

Vincent tossed me a small, black, plastic tube. "Smoke that and get some of that shit off your shoulders for right now, brother. You look like you've been through the fucking wringer."

I snorted as I popped it open and lifted the blunt to my lips. "Fucking feels like it," I admitted. "Thanks, brother."

Vincent nodded once at me before going back to what he was doing. I walked over to the car I'd been working on the day before, feeling myself already beginning to relax.

Whatever strain of weed Vincent had, it worked fast and was extremely relaxing. Making a mental note to ask him where he got it from later, I focused on the car in front of me, trying to keep my mind off of Randall, knowing that Genesis had him.

She would take care of him for me.

CHAPTER TEN
GENESIS

I released a low groan as I leaned my head on what was once my front door, my keys dangling from my grip. My locks had been changed, and all of my furniture was sitting on the sidewalk in front of the building. My landlord had put a note on my door that told me I had twenty-four hours to get my shit off the curb, or the city was going to pick it up and haul it to the dump, and the charges for that would be sent to me.

Fuck my life.

With a tired sigh and a sour feeling in my gut, I pulled my phone out and called Halen. We had barely established being together, and I was already having to call him for help.

I hated it with every fiber of my being.

"Genesis?" he asked, surprise in his voice. "Thought you were going to relax for the evening."

Tears clogged my throat. I was. At least, that had been my plan. But so quickly, my entire world was going to shit.

I sniffled. "Babe?" Halen said softly. The soothing tone to his voice did me in, and I sobbed, dropping down to sit on the steps that led up to what was once my apartment. "Hey, talk to me."

"I'm homeless," I cried. "All of my stuff has been put on the curb, and I have twenty-four hours to get it moved or the city is going to pick it up, and I'm going to be charged even more money," I cried. "Everything is going to shit."

"No, it's not," he told me, his voice stern yet still gentle. "Give me thirty minutes, and I'll be there, okay?"

I sniffled. I felt pathetic, but I'd just lost my home. It wasn't a good feeling.

"Okay," I croaked.

He hung up the phone. I set mine aside and dropped my face into my hands, trying to get myself together. Halen had already heard me crying over the phone, and he'd already seen me cry once – before he even knew my name. I didn't want him to see me breaking down for a second time.

I was stronger than this. I would get on my feet. I knew I would. I just had to wrap my head around the shit that my life had become first.

I looked up through tired eyes when the rumble of trucks reached my ears, one of them very familiar. Halen's familiar, black truck rolled to a stop, and he and Vincent jumped out as Brett rolled to a stop behind them in his older truck.

Halen gave instructions to Vincent and Brett before he turned and walked up the stairs to me, his eyes intent on my face.

I didn't have a chance to think or do anything before he tenderly cupped my face in his hands and slanted his lips across mine. I relaxed.

Somehow, I knew with Halen by my side, all of this shit would eventually work itself out. I would be okay.

"Come on down, babe," he told me, holding his hand out to me. I placed my hand in his, allowing him to pull me up from the stairs. Together, we walked down to the ground, my hand encased in his.

"You can store all of your things at my place until you figure out what's going on," Vincent told me as he and Brett loaded my couch into the back of Halen's truck.

"Are you sure?" I asked him as Halen dropped my hand and helped Brett grab my dining room table to load it in beside the couch.

"Yeah," Vincent told me, pulling his shirt up to wipe the sweat from his face. My eyes widened; I couldn't fucking help it. Were all of these men fucking ripped?

Halen shoved Vincent. "Put your fucking shirt down in front of my woman," he growled.

Vincent smirked at Halen. "Not my fault that she's attracted to me, brother."

Halen growled at him before grabbing a chair. Vincent looked back at me. "I'll store all of this in my shed out back. I don't use it for anything. Bought it on a spur-of-the-moment decision, but it's been sitting empty for two damn years. So, your stuff won't be in the way."

"Thank you," I told him, meaning it from the depths of my soul.

Vincent shrugged, leaning over to help Halen lift my dresser, walking it over to the back of Brett's truck. Brett hopped into the back to help pull it in. "You're family now, Genesis." He grunted. "With all of us, it's always as simple as that."

My throat clogged with more tears, and I blamed it on my life being uprooted because I was never this emotional.

But I knew the real reason. I'd grown up in foster homes. I'd never had a real family, and just this easily - all because I was with Halen - I belonged to one.

Once everything was loaded, Halen walked over to me. "Got two options for you," he told me. I looked up at him expectantly, waiting for him to elaborate on what those two options were. "You can stay at my place, or you can stay at the clubhouse. Whatever works best for you."

I fidgeted with my fingers. I was imposing; I couldn't help but feel like I was. But I felt more comfortable with Halen than I knew I would if I were staying at the clubhouse without him.

"I'll stay with you," I quietly told him.

He reached up and grabbed the back of my neck before pulling me closer to him, pressing his lips to mine. I sighed into the kiss, so thankful for him. He had no fucking idea.

He pressed his lips to my forehead before releasing me, reaching into his pocket. He took a key off, handing it to me. "Olivia is with Randall at the clubhouse. I just need you to pick him up and take him home with you. This is going to take me a while to unload. You good with that?"

"Halen, I'm fine," I assured him. I loved taking care of Randall. The little boy warmed my soul.

"Let Olivia know I'll square up with her tomorrow," he told me.

"Keep your fucking money," Brett snapped at Halen. Halen tilted his head back, glaring up at the sky as if he were seeking patience. I laughed. "Olivia will have both your head and mine if you try to pay her for watching Randall."

Halen grunted before looking down at me. "Shoot me a text when you've got him, yeah? And let me know when you make it home."

"I will," I assured him.

He pressed one more kiss to my forehead. "Drive safely," he ordered.

I smiled at him, watching as he walked over to his truck. He waited until I pulled off in my car before heading in the opposite direction.

Olivia smiled at me as Randall rushed out of the clubhouse doors, almost knocking me on my ass as he crashed against me, wrapping his arms around my legs. I laughed and knelt down, giving him a hug as well.

"Dad isn't coming to get me?" he asked.

I shook my head at him. "Dad had to help me, so he's doing that while I come get you. Is that okay?"

He nodded his head, beaming at me. "That's okay, Miss Genesis." He grabbed my hand in his as I stood up, looking at Olivia.

"Halen wanted me to tell you that he would square up with you tomorrow for watching him."

She rolled her eyes. "And you tell that man of yours that I said to keep his damn money." I laughed. "He knows better than to try to pay me. Brett and I don't want kids of our own. We love being the auntie and uncle." She shrugged. "Go on and get him home. I know he's tired. It's getting close to the time he normally gets a bath."

And we all knew Randall was a stickler for his routine.

I loaded Randall into my car after waving goodbye to Olivia. Randall chattered on about everything, and I listened attentively, remembering how he could get when he thought someone wasn't paying attention to what he had to say.

I glanced in my rearview mirror, frowning when I noticed an SUV was still following us. I hadn't thought much of it when I'd left the clubhouse considering that the clubhouse was right on the outskirts of town, but there weren't really any houses out here near Halen's.

A bad feeling settled in the pit of my stomach, and at that moment, I really fucking hated that I had Randall with me. I knew something bad was going to happen, and I didn't want Randall to be any part of it.

My face paled when I saw the SUV speeding up. I pressed my foot to the gas, but my little, beat-up Toyota wasn't a match, especially since it desperately needed an oil change and a tune-up.

The last thing I was aware of was my head slamming against the steering wheel and Randall's scream of terror.

CHAPTER ELEVEN
HALEN

I was exhausted. Genesis didn't have that many things, but Vincent's shed wasn't that big, so we had to angle everything to make all of her furniture fit inside without damaging it.

It had taken almost three fucking hours, especially since Vincent got pissed off about halfway through and stormed inside of his house to go grab a beer, leaving me and Brett to work by ourselves until he got over his pissy mood.

But that was Vincent for you. He was a pretty happy-go-lucky guy, but he also got agitated quickly.

He suffered from anxiety after serving overseas for four years in the Marine Corps., but instead of panic attacks like most people would expect, his anxiety made itself known in bursts of anger. It wasn't very often we saw it, though. He'd gone through therapy to learn to control it.

I slammed on my breaks, my seatbelt slamming into my chest when I saw Genesis's Toyota flipped on the side of the road. Smoke was coming from the engine.

Fear gripped my chest. What the fuck had happened?

"Randall?!" I yelled as I got out of the truck, my heart in my throat. Fuck. *Fuck!*

I rushed over to the car, instantly noticing that neither he nor Genesis were in the car. Blood was on the front seat, and her seatbelt was cut.

But I knew paramedics hadn't helped either of them. If they had, cops would still be on the scene.

Someone had taken them.

I pulled my phone out, calling Copper. "Halen?" he asked. I heard Ryker yelling in the background. "Quiet!" he barked. "Halen, what's up?"

"Copper, Genesis and Randall are missing," I rushed out. I looked around, forcing myself to calm down so I could take in the scene and try to figure out what the fuck happened. "Her car is upside down on the side of the road about a mile from my place. There's blood. Seatbelt's been cut, so she was dragged out. No sign of either of them." I looked at the grass, noticing tire tracks that weren't hers. "Larger vehicle pulled in behind them," I told him. "Something with all-terrain tires."

"Stay calm," Copper told me. "I'm on my way to you. I'll call the rest of the guys – get Logan to fucking track them."

Logan owned his own security company, though he normally kept it completely separate from the club, per Copper's request. But I knew he had even more means of tracking people than he used to before he opened his operations. "Is Randall's backpack at the scene?"

I looked into the car, my heart in my throat. "No. Gone," I told him. I looked more. "Her purse is, too." I ripped open the glove compartment. "All paperwork on the car is gone."

"Check the tag. Tag there?" Copper demanded. I heard his bike start.

I looked at the back of the car. "No. Fucking gone. *Fuck!*" I roared, tightening my hand around my phone. "They made sure whoever found this fucking car would have to fight to find out who the fuck it belonged to first," I growled.

"We're going to find them, Halen. Just fucking hang tight, you hear me? Don't you dare make a fucking move without the rest of us there. You'll only get yourself killed if you find them by yourself."

"Got it, Prez," I snarled. I hung up my phone, pacing up and down the road, too agitated, pissed, and worried to stand still. I'd failed my son. I'd promised him that he would never be hurt again, and I had fucking let him down.

My phone rang a minute later. With a grunt, I pulled it out, surprised to see Logan's name on my screen. "Yeah?" I grunted.

"Luck's on your fucking side today, brother," he told me. I could hear Walker in the background, talking to someone on the phone. "I put a tracking device in Randall's bag." I breathed a sigh of relief, thankful Logan thought about shit like this. "They're headed towards Texas. Walker is on the phone with Grim now. Copper gave Damon the order to get in touch with Alejandro. They're going to fucking get intercepted, brother. I'm tracking them on my laptop now. Walker and I are about two minutes from you. Copper should be there in a second."

Just as he said that, the sound of Copper's bike reached my ears, soon followed by the sound of others. "We're going to get them back, Halen, you hear me?"

"Yeah," I muttered. "Thanks, brother."

"They're family," Logan said. With that, he disconnected. I put my phone back in my pocket, watching as Copper rolled to a stop in front of me. "Walker and Logan will be here in a minute," he informed me. "Damon and Vincent are going to search the scene real quick. You and I are going to get your bike."

I hopped in my truck, following my president the last mile to my place where I quickly got on my bike, tearing out of the yard, heading back to the rest of the club members.

"What are we looking at?" Copper demanded as we rolled to a stop.

"We'll hit the interstate – head south," Logan told us. "We're going to have to fucking fly to reach them."

"Not a problem. I've already got the police scanner pulled up," Walker told us. "Grim is headed north with the Texas charter."

"Alejandro has gathered his men, as well as the Sons of Hell, and they're headed North as well," Damon informed us. He looked at me. "We're getting them back, Halen."

I nodded once. "We good to roll out?" I asked, not wanting to dwell here a second longer. The longer we waited to get a move on. The farther my son and my woman got away from me.

Copper nodded once. We fell into formation, Logan in our ears, keeping us up to date as we tore through the miles separating me from my son and Genesis.

Whoever took them from me would fucking pay, and it would be bloody as hell.

CHAPTER TWELVE
GENESIS

"Mom," I didn't even correct Randall as he whispered to me, his voice trembling, "are we going to be okay?"

I didn't fucking know. I had no idea what was going to happen. I was fighting to stay conscious. My head was spinning and throbbing. My entire body ached. But Randall was fine - not a single scratch or bruise that I could see - for which I was thankful.

"We're going to be just fine," I assured him, holding him close to me, glaring at his father in the driver's seat. I recognized the man from the very beginning of the year during open house where all the students and parents came to meet the teachers.

"Do you want to play a game?" I quietly asked him, desperate to keep him calm and grounded.

"What kind of game?" he asked me.

"Do you know how to play *iSpy*?" I asked him, brushing my hand over his hair before I pressed my lips to the top of his head.

He nodded. "Daddy plays it with me all the time," he whispered, keeping his voice low. The man next to us grunted in disgust. I didn't even look up at him, instead keeping my gaze focused on the little boy in my arms.

I would keep him safe, or dammit, I would fucking die trying.

I would not let him or Halen down.

"Alright." I tightened my arms around him as we drove over a bridge. "I spy something green," I told him.

He looked out the window, watching everything that passed in the lights of the headlights. "The tree?" he asked me.

"Nope." I smiled down at him, glad this was keeping him calm. I was terrified to know what would happen if he started panicking in this situation. "Try again."

"The grass?" he asked me.

I laughed quietly. "No, baby. Try again."

He looked down at my shirt which had a grass stain on it from when I got dragged out of my car. He beamed and pointed at my shirt. I smiled and nodded my head. "Good job. You're very smart," I praised.

My stomach twisted into knots as the sign for Texas popped up. I clutched Randall tighter to me, terrified of where the fuck we were going to be taken.

I screeched, and Randall clutched me tighter as the SUV came to a screeching halt in front of a bunch of expensive, top-of-the-line, black SUVs. Automatic rifles were aimed towards us. I trembled, holding Randall so tightly that I was afraid I might crush his little body, but he only clutched at me just as tightly, his entire body shaking.

"Just close your eyes, baby," I whispered. "Just close them and keep them closed, okay?"

He nodded, squeezing his eyes shut.

Randall's father got out. "What the fuck?!" he shouted.

"Give us the woman and the boy," a man with olive skin and black hair spoke, his hands in the pockets of his slacks. His eyes were dark and unnerving, but for some reason, I had a feeling he wasn't the enemy – not for me and Randall, anyway.

"Like hell!" Randall's father shouted. Randall whimpered. I gently rocked him. "He's *my* son!"

"I don't like repeating myself," the stranger warned. "Do not make me."

I squeaked in shock when the man next to me ripped Randall from my arms as I was yanked out of the door. Randall screamed, his panicked eyes meeting mine. I tried grabbing him, but I was slung out of the SUV, Randall's father using my body as a shield.

The man in front of us heaved a heavy, annoyed sigh. "I have men surrounding you," he informed us, almost as if he were bored with this entire situation. I swallowed thickly. My heart was hammering painfully against my breastbone. "Your front may be protected, but your back and your sides are not."

I trembled, squeaking in fear when a gun was suddenly pressed to my temple. I swallowed down vomit. "Wait!" I shouted, Randall's panicked screams still ringing around us. "J-just give them Randall," I pleaded with the man holding me as a shield. "You'll let them go, right?" I asked the man in front of us. He just studied me before nodding. I relaxed some. "Just let him have Randall."

The man growled. "He's my son," he snarled.

"Do you want to die here or do you want to live?" I snapped, squeaking in fear when he shoved the gun against my temple even more.

"Give him the boy!" Randall's father ordered.

I watched as the man that had snatched Randall from me carried the terrified boy over to the men with automatic rifles. I was shoved back into the SUV, but I didn't make a sound.

Randall was safe. I didn't give a shit about anything else.

The sound of motorcycles reached my ears, coming from both directions. Randall's father roared in rage, and he pointed his gun at me. I squeezed my eyes shut, my heart thumping hard in my chest. Randall screamed my name.

A gunshot rang out followed by another. A bullet tore through my thigh. I screamed in pain, my eyes flashing open as I watched Randall's father fall to the ground, blood pouring from his skull.

Two more gunshots rang through the air. Between the pain in my skull and the pain in my thigh, I fell backward on the seat, the world going dark around me, the pain pulling me under.

CHAPTER THIRTEEN
HALEN

By the time we pulled up to the scene, Alejandro's men were already wrapping bodies up in plastic. Alejandro was holding my son on his hip, but Genesis was nowhere to be seen.

I rushed over to them, and Alejandro immediately handed Randall to me. Randall clung to me, sobs wracking his chest. "Where's Genesis?" I demanded.

"Over here," Grim called. I rushed over to the back of their club van. Medic was working on pulling a bullet out of Genesis's thigh, and she was unconscious.

"She's going to need a hospital," Medic told me. "But I need to get this bleeding stopped first. There's some swelling to the front and back of her head. Good thing that it's outward, but head injuries are still tricky."

I swallowed vomit. This wasn't supposed to happen to her – to either of them.

"Your woman is a brave one," Alejandro told me, stuffing his hands into his pockets. I didn't rip my eyes from Genesis's pale face. "She was able to get Randall's father to give Randall over to me. I saw the acceptance in her eyes. She was willing to die to save your son."

"She's incredible," I rasped, clutching Randall tighter to me. I could have lost both of them today.

"She's one of a kind," Alejandro said quietly. "If I were you, I'd do everything in my power to keep her."

I nodded once. "Working on it," I told him.

Medic stood back and ripped his gloves off as Scab began putting Medic's equipment away. "We'll get her to the nearest hospital," Grim told me. "Go on and head there," he ordered Medic. "I'll catch Copper up on everything so he can let you know."

I nodded once. "We'll bring your bike to my clubhouse," Grim said I strode around to the passenger side of the van. I hadn't even thought about my bike. As soon as I'd laid my eyes on Randall, everything else but Genesis had faded from my mind. "Come collect it whenever you can."

I grunted a thanks before I slid into the passenger seat, Medic sliding into the driver's. Randall leaned his head back, looking up at me through his teary eyes. "Is Mom going to be okay?"

My heart clenched in my chest. He was already so fucking attached to her, just as I was.

"She's going to be okay, buddy," I soothed, reaching up to wipe some tears from his face. Genesis was too fucking strong to allow this to take her out. "She's just resting."

He sniffled, reaching up to wipe his nose with his jacket sleeve. "She played *iSpy* with me."

Of course, she fucking did. Despite them being in such a dangerous situation, she still did whatever she could to keep him grounded – to make him feel safe.

I'd never be able to repay her for this, and I'd never be able to make up this shit to her either.

A groan sounded from the back of the van. I turned my head, watching as Genesis slowly sat up, her hand coming up to touch her head before she released a low whine of pain.

"Easy, baby," I soothed. She slowly turned to look at me. I set Randall on the floor of the van before I got up and moved toward her. Her eyes were a bit hazy and unfocused. "You've got a hell of a head injury."

"Where's Randall?" she moaned as Medic hit a bump in the road, making pain flash across her face.

"Right here," Randall announced his presence, crawling across the floor towards her. She breathed a sigh of relief, wrapping him up in her arms.

"You're safe. You're okay," she breathed, tears sliding down her cheeks.

I cupped the side of her neck, brushing my thumb over her jaw. "You did so, so fucking good, baby," I praised. "You kept him safe." I swallowed thickly. "Thank you."

She nodded, her eyes sliding shut, her body slumping. I quickly caught her, holding her to me as she went unconscious again. Randall slid his panicked eyes over her face, but I wrapped my other arm around him. "Easy, kiddo. She's sleeping again, okay?" I sort of lied. "Her head hurts really bad."

He nodded, resting his head on my shoulder, his hands grabbing one of hers in both of his. He didn't remove his eyes from her face. A frown pulled at his lips, but he trusted my word that she would be okay.

I just hoped and prayed that I was right and that my words wouldn't become a full lie.

When we got to the hospital, Genesis was immediately taken into the back as I filled out her paperwork to the best of my ability. I did a lot of pacing after Randall finally passed out in a chair in her room.

Her CT scan results came back fine. She would be placed in a small coma until the swelling in her head was reduced some. I could expect her to be awake in two to three days, depending on how long it took.

But there was no trauma to her brain. All of the swelling was on the outside, but the doctor wanted to take extra precautions, which I didn't mind.

I'd rather be too cautious than not cautious enough. She meant too fucking much to me to ever be otherwise.

I got updates from Copper, letting me know the scene had been cleaned up and that Vincent and Logan were bringing my truck to the hospital and grabbing my bike from Grim's to take it back to my house.

I didn't know what the fuck I would do without this club – without this brotherhood that I was part of.

Three days later, Genesis was pulled out of the coma, and I was left waiting on her to naturally wake up on her own. Randall read to her every day that she was unconscious.

Copper and Penny had offered to take him home and take care of him while I was with Genesis, but I had shut that down fast. I wasn't ready for Randall to be out of my sight yet, and honestly, I didn't think my little boy was all that keen on being parted from me, either.

A few hours after she was pulled out of the coma, her eyes slowly fluttered open. She stared at the ceiling for a couple of minutes before turning her head, her eyes latching onto mine. I smiled at her, so fucking glad to finally see her awake.

"Hey, babe," I greeted. I gently cupped her bruised face in my hands and pressed my lips to hers. "Good to finally see you awake."

"Where am I?" she croaked.

I poured her a cup of water and placed the straw at her lips. She slowly drank all of the water as I answered her. "You're in a hospital," I told her. "You were shot, not to mention you had some pretty bad swelling on the front and back of your head."

"The accident," she told me. She licked her lips, her eyes shutting for a moment before she opened them again. "I hit my head on the steering wheel really hard."

I nodded. "Looks like they banged you up pretty good when they were pulling you out of the car, too," I admitted. I brushed the back of my fingers over her cheek. "But you're expected to make a full recovery."

"Randall?" she asked me.

I smiled down at her, loving how concerned she was for our little boy. And he was *ours*. After what she had done for him, she *deserved* the title of Mom.

"He's taking a nap." I moved aside so she could see him curled up in the reclining chair beside her bed. "He's been reading to you every day – said you like books."

She weakly smiled, still looking so exhausted. "I do." She yawned. "I'm tired."

I leaned over and gently brushed my lips to hers. "Will you be okay if I let the doctor know you're awake? Can you stay up that long?"

She shut her eyes. "I'll try," she whispered.

I quickly walked out of the room since hers was right across from the nurse's station and let them know that she was awake, but if the doctor wanted to see her, he needed to hurry since she was still pretty tired.

After seeing the doctor, he scheduled another CT scan to check the swelling. After getting the results from that, he ordered a minimum of two more nights in the hospital just to keep an eye on her thigh and her head trauma, and then after that, he would decide whether to let her go home or not.

CHAPTER FOURTEEN
GENESIS

I limped over to Halen's truck after work. Two weeks had passed since I had finally been released from the hospital. Randall was back in school and back in his normal routine, though he and Ryker were having a sleepover, giving me and Halen some much-needed time to ourselves.

Halen had barely let us out of his sights in the fear that something else would happen to us. I understood it, but the overprotective thing that he had going on with me was wearing on my last fucking nerve. I felt like I could barely shit in peace anymore before he was knocking on the door, asking me if I was okay.

I tried to deal with it as much as I could considering every other night, Halen was waking up in a cold sweat, his face pale as he relived the fear that he had felt when he'd found my car on the side of the road.

I hated seeing such a strong man have his entire fucking world shaken like he had – to see him relive that shit in his mind almost every single night.

I squeaked in shock when Halen suddenly gripped my waist and lifted me into the passenger seat of his truck. Then, leaning in, his hands on either side of my hips, he leaned in and took my lips in a hot, possessive kiss that had me moaning – fucking *craving* him.

"That'll hold until we get home," he rumbled, brushing his lips to my jaw before he stepped back from me and shut the truck door, walking around the front of the truck to hop in on the driver's side.

We were halfway to his place when he suddenly pulled off onto a narrow dirt road and grabbed me, lifting me onto his lap.

I ground against him, unable to help myself. I'd taken my pain medicine before leaving work, so the pain in my thigh was barely there. "Are we really about to have hot as fuck sex in your truck like we're teenagers?" I asked him.

He laced his fingers in my hair. "Damn fucking right, we are," he growled. "I fucking need you, Genesis, and I can't fucking wait until we get home to have you."

I shoved my hands under his shirt, my lips meeting his. He took control, his hands sliding into my stretchy shorts to slide along my pussy. I moaned his name, grinding against his rough hand.

Fuck, Halen felt *amazing*.

"Yes, baby," he growled. He yanked my head back, his lips running down my neck, his teeth scraping my skin. "Take what you fucking need, Genesis."

I moaned, fucking his fingers, the rough heel of his hand rubbing against my clit. My body shuddered, and his name fell from my lips on a soft cry as I came around him.

With his help, I shimmied out of my shorts. Lucky for both of us, I was wearing a thong. He pulled a condom on before pulling my thong to the side and sinking deep inside of me. Both of us moaned at the feeling before he hooked my legs around him and began rocking me back and forth, putting less pressure on my thigh, but still hitting that perfect spot inside of me as he did so.

I came hard around him, but he still didn't stop, his lips working with mine as he rocked me faster, drawing me over the edge numerous times before he finally came as well, holding me to him as we waited for our heartrates to slow back to normal.

His phone rang, the sound jarring us both. Halen released a long groan before grabbing his phone. "What, Copper?" he growled. His eyes widened. "Fuck; yeah. We're on our way."

He hung up. With his help, I got back into the passenger seat and pulled my shorts back on as he fixed his clothes, putting his cock back in his boxers.

"Randall is having a meltdown," Halen told me as he pulled back onto the main highway, speeding towards Copper's. "He's crying for me."

"Fuck," I whispered. And we had been roughnecking in his truck like horny teenagers while his son was becoming overwhelmed.

Halen grabbed my hand in his, easily navigating the streets through town before pulling up at Penny and Copper's. He jumped out of the truck, rushing inside. I eased down and limped towards the house. When I walked in, Halen was sitting on the couch with Randall wrapped around him. I took a seat beside them, reaching up to run my hand over Randall's hair.

"Mom isn't leaving again, is she?" Randall sniffled. Ever since that tragic day, I'd been Mom to Randall. And we'd never bothered to correct him. Honestly, it warmed my soul to know that Randall looked to me as a mom.

"I never left, baby," I soothed. He looked over at me through his glassy eyes.

"But you did," he whimpered. "You were asleep for so long. I don't want you to leave me again."

"Hey, your mom is never leaving you," Halen soothed, reaching up to brush the tears from Randall's eyes. "Nothing like that will ever happen to her again, you hear me?" I felt like he was saying those words not just for Randall but for me, too.

"You promise, Dad?" Randall croaked.

Halen nodded. "I promise, kiddo."

He stood from the couch. Penny handed me a large to-go container of food. She smiled at me. "Dinner is on us tonight," she told me. "I'm sorry that you guys didn't get the alone time you wanted."

This was the kind of family I'd wanted to belong in all my life – the kind that sent you home with food, watched your kid for you, the kind that was always there for you, no matter the circumstances.

I hugged her. "Don't worry about it. Randall is more important to us than a night by ourselves."

She squeezed me before releasing me. Copper nodded once at me before I followed Halen out of the house, putting the to-go container of food in the backseat.

Randall was asleep before we even got to the house. Not wanting to wake him, Halen just carried him inside up to his room, laying him in bed with Django.

"Are you hungry?" Halen asked me as I put the food into the fridge.

I shook my head. "I can't stomach anything after that," I admitted. I leaned against the kitchen counter, crossing my arms over my chest. "I hate that I wasn't stronger that day. Yeah, I kept him safe, but now he's living with the constant fear that something is going to happen to me."

Halen wrapped me up in his arms, tucking my head under his chin. "He just needs some time, baby." He smoothed his hand over my hair. "Come on. Let's go upstairs. He'll be asleep for a while. It's going to be a strange night since he went to bed so early."

I nodded in agreement. He would probably wake up around midnight, and we would all eat dinner together before he got a shower and we put him to bed again.

Once we were upstairs in our bedroom, Halen kissed me, his tongue sliding against mine. I moaned into the kiss, my hands tangling in his hair.

His hands clasped my waist as he gently led me back to the bed, his steps slow and steady as I limped, our lips still working together, becoming more and more heated and demanding.

Once I was on the bed, Halen stripped me out of my clothes, his lips and tongue running all over my body as he did so. I was a writhing, panting mess by the time he buried his face between my legs, sliding the flat of his tongue between my folds before roughly sliding his tongue against my clit. I moaned, tangling my fingers in his hair as I began to ride his face, trying to keep myself as quiet as possible so I wouldn't wake the little boy down the hall.

Halen reached up and clamped his hand over my mouth as I came so I wouldn't wake up Randall. Then, he stood up and quickly removed his clothes before pulling on a condom and sliding deep inside of me, slowly rocking us together as he made sweet, slow love to me.

"I love you, Genesis," he rasped, burying his head into the curve of my neck.

Hot tears slid down my cheeks. I clutched at his back. "Oh, God, Halen, I love you, too," I cried.

And I did. I was hopelessly in love with this demanding man. Despite my fears of attaching myself to him and despite him being so fucking stubborn and hardheaded, I was so, so fucking deeply in love with him that it rattled me straight to my core.

But I knew I wouldn't change it for a damn thing. I would forever want this man – would forever crave him as mine.

CHAPTER FIFTEEN
HALEN

I swallowed thickly as I stared down at the papers in my hands. Emotion clogged my throat as tears blurred my vision.

I was officially Randall's father. The adoption had been finalized today on Randall's eighth birthday.

Drake clapped his hand to my shoulder as we stood outside of the courthouse. "Well, Halen, you're officially a dad now. How's it feel?"

"Fucking unreal," I admitted. "Holy fucking shit."

Drake barked out a laugh. "You've done a fucking amazing job so far with him, Halen. You're going to do even better as he gets older."

I looked over at my brother. "You going to be able to make it to his birthday party this weekend?" I asked him.

Drake nodded. "I wouldn't miss it for the world, bro." He looked at his watch with a heavy sigh. "Fuck. I have to go do paperwork. Shoot me a text with the time, yeah?"

He walked off to his car, pulling his phone from his pocket. I sent Genesis a text, telling her to bring Randall in the truck to the clubhouse. I'd gotten her a Raptor a month ago so she would have her own personal vehicle.

That had been a fucking fight. She'd almost broken up with me – felt like I was doing too much for her – but like fuck was I letting that woman walk away from me.

I'd slung her over my shoulder and carried her upstairs, making love to her until I got it through her thick ass skull that I did this kind of shit because I loved her, and I wanted her to have the very best, not a damn other reason.

She called me as I was getting on my bike. "Yeah, babe?" I asked as I strapped my helmet to my head.

"Randall is with Alejandro, remember?" she asked me.

Fuck; I'd forgotten. Randall had grown a strange attachment to the dangerous man, but I knew Randall was safe with Alejandro.

The man had saved my son and my woman's life.

"Fuck. Yeah; I forgot. Today has been crazy." I sighed. "I'll be home in a little bit."

"So, you don't need me to come to the clubhouse?" she asked me.

"Nah," I told her. "But I do want you at home in that sexy ass lingerie I know you bought with Olivia when y'all went shopping."

I knew Genesis was blushing. "I'm hanging up, Halen."

I barked out a laugh. "See you in a few, baby."

I hung up the call and pulled out of the courthouse parking lot, heading home to give my woman the good news and have hot, sweaty, celebratory sex.

Genesis was sitting on the couch eating a bowl of ice cream when I walked inside. I'd specifically asked Kyle to give her today off with me. He'd looked at me funny but had granted it anyway.

"Hey," she greeted, setting her bowl on the table. "What's that?" she asked, looking at the papers in my hands.

I walked over and handed them to her. She eyed me curiously but took them from me, looking down at them.

I watched as her eyes widened, a wide grin crossing her face. She launched herself off the couch at me, her arms and legs wrapping around me. I laughed, gripping her ass in my hands as I stumbled but kept us from falling to the floor.

"Halen, this is amazing!" she gushed, leaning back a little to grab my face in her hands. She kissed me deeply, her tongue tangling with mine.

I groaned and pressed her back against the nearest wall, my hand sliding under her shirt. Shoving her bra cup down some, I grabbed her breast in my hand, deepening the kiss.

She moaned just as the front door flew open. I quickly set her down, reaching for my gun as Genesis quickly righted herself right before Randall and Alejandro walked in the door.

"Fuck," I swore. I pressed a kiss to Genesis's forehead before swooping Randall into a hug. "You're home early, kid."

"Alejandro said he had to do something, and he said I couldn't go with him."

Probably a good choice. God only knew what in the hell Alejandro had to go take care of, and I didn't want my son to be a part of it.

Alejandro nodded once at me, his eyes flickering to the papers on the coffee table. With a small tilt to his lips, he inclined his head to me before leaving without a word, shutting the front door behind him.

Randall moved away from me, walking over to the coffee table where the papers were. I grabbed Genesis's hand in mine, linking our fingers together as I watched Randall read them.

"Dad?" he asked me, looking up at me, excitement brimming in his eyes. I swallowed thickly. "Is this real? Are you my real dad now?"

"Yeah, kiddo," I rasped. "I'm your real dad now." Though in my mind, since the moment I brought him into my home, he had been my son - blood be damned.

He launched himself at me, and I dropped to the floor, wrapping him up in my arms. We stayed like that for a good minute, his hug like a vice around my neck, but I didn't care.

He was finally going to be my son completely. No one could take him from me, which had been my biggest fear while I was waiting on the adoption papers to go through.

Randall leaned back to look at me. "So, when is she going to become my forever mom?" he asked, pointing his finger at Genesis.

I grinned at her, watching as her cheeks flamed red at his question. I winked at him. "Soon, kiddo," I told him, ruffling his hair, a teasing note to my voice. I knew he was getting impatient. He was dying for me to marry Genesis, but I wanted it to be special for both of them.

And I didn't want to give either of them any kind of hint that I was planning on popping the question soon.

But I had every intention of making this woman mine in every way I possibly could.

I lifted my bottle to my lips, watching as Genesis laughed at something Skylar said. Kyle stood next to me with their son on his hip.

"Your kid is getting impatient. He wants to open his gifts," he told me, laughing as Randall tried sneaking towards the table, but Genesis caught him, pointing her finger away from him.

He just innocently smiled at her before darting away to go play with Ryker.

Genesis and I, along with everyone else, had gotten Randall a shit ton of gifts. It was his first birthday with us, and from what I understood, it was the first time he ever actually got to celebrate it.

I knew the only thing he really wanted was for me to marry Genesis so she could finally be his forever mom, as he called it, so, besides all of his presents, that was going to be a gift to him as well.

"You're helping me clean all of this shit up," I told Kyle as I set my beer aside, getting ready to go let Randall open his gifts.

Kyle scoffed. "Like hell."

I shrugged. "Suit yourself, but I'll bring it back up in a couple of years when you're needing help cleaning up after one of his birthday parties," I told him, pointing at his son.

Kyle grunted. "Fucking fine."

I grinned triumphantly and walked over to the table, pausing for a moment to press a kiss to Genesis's lips.

I'd never seen Randall so excited before in my life. He ripped open his gifts, shouting excitedly with each one, happily posing for each picture that Genesis took of him. He even laughed when I smashed a little bit of cake in his face.

He was having a fucking blast, and honestly, I couldn't have been happier. I was a little worried today might be too much for him, but so far, he was soaking it all up.

I waited until Genesis was done wiping his face clean before I got down on one knee. Instantly, the clubhouse fell quiet. Frowning, Genesis stood up and looked around before her eyes fell on me.

She squeaked in shock, her hands flying up to her face, getting cake on her face from the towel as she did so.

I rolled my lips into my mouth to keep from laughing, though my cock stirred in my jeans at the thought of licking that cake off of her skin.

Focus, Halen.

I drew in a deep breath, pulling the big-ass diamond ring from my pocket. I knew I had gone way overboard with the ring, but fuck, this woman of mine deserved the absolute best. She had protected my son, giving her a permanent limp as she did so. She lost her dream job trying to get him help.

I could give her everything in the fucking world, and it *still* wouldn't be enough.

"Genesis, I knew from the moment you told me that you lost your job trying to help a little boy that you were the one for me," I told her. She set the towel down, her hands shaking. Randall grabbed her hand in his, his eyes locked on me as well. "I came from a shit home. I wouldn't even be alive today if it weren't for Copper taking me in and forcing me to get my shit together." I drew in a deep breath. "To find a woman so fiercely protective over a little boy, to see her more upset over the fact that he would still be trapped than she was over her job – fuck, babe, it was like you punched me in my fucking gut."

Two tears slid down her cheek. She reached up and shakily swiped them away. "From that day on, I knew I would never fucking let you get away from me. And when I saw how good you were with Randall, saw how much he adored you, I fell even harder for you."

My eyes flickered to Randall for a brief moment. He was clutching Genesis's hand so tightly that his knuckles were white.

"I have never been more terrified in my life than I was the day I found your car on the side of the road, blood everywhere, and you both were missing. I panicked. Me - someone who always has his fucking shit together - fucking panicked. But babe, you didn't. You kept your shit together, forcing yourself to stay conscious to keep Randall safe. You were ready to die that day if it meant he got to live and that he got to safety."

She was crying so hard now that she couldn't wipe the tears away fast enough. "I love you, Genesis. I want to spend the rest of my life giving you everything I fucking can. I don't know what in the hell I was doing with my life before you stepped into it, but it obviously wasn't shit." Laughter bubbled up in her chest. She sniffled. "I want to marry you, Genesis. Will you please do me the fucking amazing honor of becoming my wife - of becoming Randall's forever mom?"

"Yes," she croaked. "A thousand times fucking yes, Halen."

I jumped up from the floor and dragged her into my arms, kissing her so deeply that it honestly should have been reserved for the bedroom - or at least away from my son's eyes - but at that moment, I didn't care.

The woman of my fucking dreams had just agreed to marry me.

Cheers erupted in the clubhouse. I slid the ring on her finger before I reluctantly released her, lifting Randall into my arms. He threw his arms around Genesis's neck, and she broke down sobbing, holding him tightly as well.

This was what I'd been missing my entire fucking life.

CHAPTER SIXTEEN
GENESIS

I sighed in annoyance when my phone rang on the office desk. I'd just gotten off the phone with an extremely rude customer that was extremely pissed that his part hadn't come in. It was so bad that Damon had to come in and take the call, threatening to undo all the work he'd done so far and having him come pick up his vehicle to take to a different shop.

The man's attitude towards me had quickly changed, but it hadn't made me any less weary and exhausted.

To top it off, it wasn't even fucking lunch time yet.

I picked my phone up when it started ringing, and I frowned at the board of education's number. Anxiety swirled in my gut. I honestly debated on letting it go to voicemail, but I swiped my finger across the screen at the very last second, answering it.

"Hello. May I speak to Genesis Carmichael?"

"This is her," I hesitantly spoke, setting my pen down. "How can I help you?"

"Hi, Miss Carmichael. This is the superintendent with the board of education, Betty Wright. I'm calling to inform you that we would love to have you return as a teacher in the fall, if you are open to that."

A surprised breath of air left my lips at her words. I had never expected to get my teaching job back. I missed the children so much, but I had finally come to terms with the fact that I would no longer be a teacher.

And now it was being offered to me again?

"Um, yes, of course," I rushed out. "Do I need to come fill out any paperwork?"

"Not unless your marital status, place of address, banking information, etc. has changed," she told me. "If it has, you can access your profile online through the school board website and change all of your information there."

"Okay. I will do that," I told her. "Thank you again."

"Of course, Miss Carmichael. Have a wonderful day."

I hung up the call and got out of my chair, going to find Halen. I *knew* he had something to do with this. Every time I had brought up my teaching job the last few weeks, he had shut the conversation down, almost as if he didn't want to listen to it.

"Halen Anderson!" I shouted. A tool fell to the floor as everyone turned their heads to look at me. My fiancé rolled out from under a car, sitting up to look at me. "Get in the fucking office!" I barked, turning on my heel to storm back inside of the airconditioned room.

"What the hell did you do this time?" I heard Walker ask him.

I heard Halen sigh. "Who the fuck knows," he grumbled. He stepped into the office a moment later. He had a grease stain on his cheek and one above his brow. His hands were dirty, and he smelled like sweat and oil.

Fuck, why did it make me want to jump his fucking bones? A normal woman would be repulsed. But nope, not me. I was turned the fuck on.

I planted my hands on my hips, glaring at him. "I just received a call from the school board," I seethed. "They offered me my teaching position back."

He pulled a towel from his pocket and wiped his hands on it. "I hope you took it."

"Of course, I did," I snapped. He arched an eyebrow at me. "Did you have something to do with that?" I demanded.

He nodded, never one to lie to me. "Yep." He even had the audacity to pop the *p*. I wanted to smack him. "Once the adoption was finalized, I got the club attorney to fight for your position back. Now that your position has been offered to you, she'll begin working on getting everyone who ignored your reports fired, as it's actually against the law for them to ignore reports of child abuse. What they fucking did to both you and Randall was wrong, and I don't want it happening to another teacher or another student."

I sighed, my anger deflating. How could I be mad at him when he explained it like that? "I told you I was going to get it taken care of."

He leaned back against the wooden door, his eyes intent on my face. "Genesis, I know you're eyeballs deep in student debt still, not to mention your credit card bills from trying to keep yourself afloat after you lost your teaching position." I winced. "That doesn't allow you much room to pay for an attorney." He shrugged. "If you'd let me make the payments for the Raptor and the insurance, it would, but you're a stubborn as fuck, independent woman."

I couldn't help it. I smiled. He sounded so aggravated and disgruntled. He rolled his eyes. "Of course, that would make you smile," he grumbled.

I sighed. "I know I'm bitchy about everything, but thank you." He just smiled at me. "I'm thankful and grateful; I really am. I just wish you would stop coddling me so much."

He rolled his eyes again. "Babe, it's not coddling. I'm taking care of you. I love you." He walked forward and cupped my face in his dirty hands. "I take care of what's mine." He pressed a kiss to the tip of my nose. "Just let me do that, yeah? You sit back, make whatever money you want to make," he rolled his eyes heavenward, making me giggle, "pay your fucking truck and insurance payments," I burst into laughter, "and let me take care of everything else, yeah? Between the club and the garage, I make more than enough, baby."

I sighed. "I hate relying on anyone."

He shrugged. "Get used to it, babe. I'm not going anywhere."

He kissed me, his lips soft and soothing against mine. I moaned, opening my lips beneath his. He growled, pushing me against the desk.

"No office sex," I breathlessly told him.

"Fuck," he groaned, rolling his head back on his shoulders to stare at the ceiling.

I smirked and dropped to my knees. "But there is this," I whispered as I dropped to my knees. I unzipped his coveralls and pulled his dick out of his shorts.

He moaned, tangling his fingers in my hair as I sucked him deep into my mouth, relaxing my gag reflex. I allowed him to fuck my mouth, loving it when he took control like this.

It wasn't long before he was coming down my throat, his cum tasting a bit salty. I swallowed it all, popping him out of my mouth afterward.

"Better?" I asked him.

He grinned and helped me up to my feet before leaning in and kissing me. "Your pussy would have been better, but that'll hold me until we get home."

I laughed at him. He grinned and stepped back from me, adjusting himself before he shot me a wink and walked out of the office.

CHAPTER SEVENTEEN
HALEN

I bent over to look closer at what one of our repeat customers was showing me on his car. He'd bought yet another piece of shit car to fix and resell.

Didn't matter to me. His piece of shit cars put money on my paycheck.

"That's your serpentine belt and water pully," I told him. "Gonna have to replace both. Radiator hoses are shot. Probably need a new radiator as well." I looked over at him. "By the time I get done with this, you're basically going to have a brand new engine."

He shrugged. "You guys do the best work. Whatever it is, let me know. I'll have the money to you as soon as you give me a grand total."

"Got it," I told him, shaking his hand as I stood back up.

He moved towards the office. I reached up to close the hood. Something popped and hit me in my back. With a growl, I turned around. Genesis was standing there with a laughing Randall, and Logan and Vincent were the culprits holding confetti cannons. Blue and pink confetti settled down around me.

"What the fuck?" I demanded.

Genesis walked towards me, handing me some kind of folded, glossy paper. With a sigh, I unfolded it, my eyes widening at the pictures.

She was pregnant.

I snapped my eyes up to hers. She suddenly looked unsure, her eyes nervously running over my face.

"You're pregnant?" I breathed.

She nervously tucked her white-blonde hair behind her ear and nodded. Grinning, I wrapped an arm around the back of her neck and dragged her to me, slanting my lips across hers.

It was all out of fucking order, considering I wanted to marry her before we brought another kid into the household, but now that she was pregnant, I didn't want it any other way.

Fuck, just the thought of her being pregnant with a big, round belly fucking turned me the hell on.

"What a way to ruin the wedding, babe," I teased, my lips brushing hers.

She blushed and shrugged her shoulders. "We can either rush the wedding or push it further back," she told me. "That's entirely up to you."

"Mmm . . . we'll push it off," I told her. "You don't need the added stress of teaching plus trying to plan a wedding on top of preparing for a baby." I brushed my nose with hers. "You're going to be a hot as fuck pregnant woman."

She smacked my shoulder. I laughed. "Wait, Mom is pregnant?!" Randall yelled in excitement.

Genesis moved back from me. Randall rushed forward, launching himself into my arms. I lifted him up. "Yes, she's pregnant. Is that okay with you, bud?"

He eagerly nodded his head. I knew he loved the idea, but the real test would be when his routine was messed up when the baby came. He was getting a lot better about certain things, but his routine was still something that was a trigger.

He *needed* order. It wasn't an option for him.

But like Genesis and I always did, we would take it one day at a time, soothing him into a new routine.

The guys instantly began congratulating me. Skylar threw her arms around Genesis, almost knocking her to the ground, but Genesis caught herself in time.

"I'm so fucking happy for you!" Skylar yelled.

Damon clapped my back. "Fatherhood looks good on you, brother. You've come a long way from that fucked up kid Copper found."

His words meant more to me than he would ever know. "Thanks, brother."

"Dad, is it going to hurt Mom to have a baby?" Randall asked me.

I looked down at Randall. "It will," I told him honestly. "But I promise, it's a small price that she has to pay to give you a little brother or sister."

"I want a little sister - like Mom," Randall told me, actually surprising me. "Ryker says girls suck," that caused a round of laughter, "but Mom is really nice, and she loves me a lot. Will my sister love me, too?"

Fuck, I loved this kid.

"If you have a little sister, Randall, she will love you just as much as your mom does. Granted, she might get mad at you a lot—"

"Like Mom does you?" he asked.

I barked out a laugh. "Yes, kiddo, like she does me, but she will always love you."

He nodded. Ryker dragged him away as I set him on his feet. Copper clapped a hand to my shoulder. "You've done fucking wonders with him, Halen. He's grown so much since he came into your care."

I looked over at him. "I learned from the best," I told him honestly.

Copper shook his head. "No, Halen. I just showed you that being a low-life piece of shit wasn't all it was cut out to be." I snorted. "The moment I met you, I knew you were capable of doing better things. Just had to get you right first."

I watched as Genesis quickly took a tool from Randall, gently reprimanding him since he knew it was a rule that he couldn't touch any of the tools without adult supervision.

Randall pouted, the first he had ever done so. He stomped away from her, and suddenly, Genesis began to cry. My eyes widened in alarm. I rushed over and drew her into my arms. I knew it was a stage Randall was going through and one she would have to grow accustomed to.

Every day, he was coming more and more out of his shell, which meant he was also beginning to act more like his age.

Which meant he was going to be a brat about getting his way.

"All I did was take the tool." She sniffled. "And he got mad. But why am I crying?"

I pressed my lips to her temple. "It's just the pregnancy hormones, babe," I soothed, trying not to laugh. Genesis hated crying. "It only gets worse."

She wailed. "I hate this! I thought this was only a myth. I know plenty of women who don't get like this."

I hugged her tighter. "It's different for every woman," Skylar tried soothing her. "From what I understand, Penny was a mess, whereas I was just bitchy."

My eyes widened in horror. I wasn't sure if I could deal with Genesis being bitchier than normal. Copper barked out a laugh at my horrified expression.

"What?" Genesis asked, moving back from me, looking up at me. "What's wrong?"

"Nothing," I quickly answered, not wanting to set her off. I loved Genesis with every fiber of my being, but sometimes, she scared the shit out of me. She was so fiercely independent and vocal about her feelings, which was a really good thing, but she put the fear of God into me sometimes.

She narrowed her eyes at me, no longer crying. "Wait, you think I'm going to get bitchier?" she snapped at me. I cringed. She spun on her heel. "Go fuck yourself, Halen."

I sighed and grabbed her wrist, silently cursing Randall in my head for causing this emotional disaster in the first place. And then cursing my dick for turning Genesis into this beautiful mess.

"Baby, no," I soothed. She tried yanking her wrist from my grip. With a growl, I laced my fingers in her hair and yanked her lips to mine, effectively shutting her up and wiping her mind of everything she'd been fighting with me about.

Her body relaxed. Pecking her lips one last time, I pulled back. "Better?" I asked her.

"Sorry," She mumbled.

I grinned at her. "I love every part of you, babe. Even the emotional, bitchy parts."

She rolled her eyes. "Go fuck yourself, Halen."

I flashed her a wicked smirk. Her pupils dilated, her breath hitching in her throat. "Nah, babe. That's what I've got you for."

Her cheeks burned red at my words. I flashed her a grin before going to find my son to force him to apologize to Genesis. But first, I needed to give him a long talk about how we needed to handle Genesis with care or she just might bite our heads off.

CHAPTER EIGHTEEN
HALEN

Genesis groaned in agitation, glaring at Skylar who was trying to motivate my woman to get off of the couch. I wished her luck because Genesis was suffering from Braxton Hicks contractions today and didn't want to get off of the couch.

"Genesis, come *on!*" Skylar complained. I snorted, shooting two guys on the game. Randall quickly shot one, running for cover afterward. I went in search of him to protect his back. "It's your baby shower. Who doesn't show up to their own baby shower?"

"Someone who feels like shit and doesn't want to move," Genesis told her. "I appreciate the thought - I swear that I do - but I *really* don't feel good, Skylar."

And it wasn't just the Braxton Hicks contractions. Genesis was at risk of losing our baby. She *had* to stay stress-free and off her feet as much as possible.

Skylar shot her a deadpan look. "It's Braxton Hicks contractions - not labor, Genesis."

"In her defense," I said, snatching up a teammate's tags before rushing after Randall to keep him protected, "the doctor did say that Genesis's pregnancy is high risk." Which was true. When Genesis complained about the cramps she was having, the doctor did some further testing just to be on the safe side. At thirty-two weeks pregnant, her mucus plug was already thinning. She'd been put on bed rest, which meant she had to stop working a lot sooner than she had wanted.

"She can come to a baby shower, Halen," Skylar told me.

I sighed, glancing at Genesis. She frowned at me. She hadn't wanted me to tell anyone that she was on bedrest and that she was at risk of having the baby extremely early, but Skylar was being stubborn as shit.

"Tell her," Genesis told me. "Because I'm not getting up, and I know nothing short of a natural disaster will keep her from bugging the shit out of me."

I cursed when I died, officially ending the game. I turned my head to look at Randall. "Kiddo, can you go upstairs and shut your door? I'll call you back down in a minute."

He nodded and went upstairs. Once I heard his door shut, I got up and went to the kitchen, grabbing Genesis a bottle of water. "Skylar, Genesis is at risk of losing our baby," I told her when I reentered the room. Skylar's eyes widened. "She complained to the doctor about her cramping at the last appointment. She is suffering from

Braxton Hick's contractions, yes, but her mucus plug is also thinning. She's been put on bedrest." I shrugged. "No, it probably won't harm her to go to the baby shower, but it is her body, our baby, and her choice. If she doesn't want to go, no one is going to force her."

"I had no idea," Skylar whispered. "Why didn't you tell anyone?"

"I asked him not to," Genesis told her, smiling at me when I handed her the water. "I didn't want anyone worrying. The doctor said that as long as I don't do any unnecessary walking, try to rest as much as possible, and keep my stress levels to a minimum, I'll be fine, and I'll deliver a healthy baby when it's time."

"And you aren't worried about premature birth?" she asked incredulously.

Genesis shook her head. "I'm following the doctor's orders to a T." She really was, even if it was driving her nuts. "So, no, I'm not worried. And even if I do give birth early, I've been assured numerous times by my doctor that our baby will make it and grow into a very healthy child."

Skylar frowned. "I wish we had known, Genesis. I'm so sorry. I feel like such a bitch for downplaying what you're feeling."

I sighed. "Skylar, don't," I told her. "You had no idea. If it's possible, bring everyone and all of the gifts here." I looked at Genesis. "That'll be fine with you, right, babe?"

She smiled at Skylar. "Of course. You guys went through a lot to throw this for me. I feel horrible for not going but—"

"Your health is more important," Skylar told her, cutting her off. "Let me call Penny, Olivia, and Cassidy. We'll bring it here. The kids can play outside while you guys open your gifts. That sound okay?"

Genesis nodded. Skylar hugged her before leaving, pulling her phone from her pocket. Genesis frowned once she left. "I feel so horrible for not going to enjoy everything they've done for me."

I leaned over her and pressed a kiss to the top of her head. "Don't feel bad, baby. You have to take care of yourself first."

She smiled up at me. "You're incredible."

I leaned over the couch again, gently pressing my lips to hers. "So are you, babe."

I stared in astonishment at the baby's room. I'd been planning to paint this for a few weeks now but had kept putting it off.

And now, it was done, and all of my brothers were standing in the room. All of the furniture had been put together and organized, all of the clothes put away.

"Shit," I breathed, feeling a bit overwhelmed. "You guys didn't have to do this."

"We wanted to," Copper told me. "We didn't realize you and Genesis were going through so much."

I shrugged. "It's not really that much," I said, though it was. Her mucus plug had fallen out the night before, though I hadn't told anyone that. She was thirty-four weeks pregnant. I was terrified as fuck, but I was forcing myself to be brave for her. She had an appointment in a couple of hours, hence why I was up so damn early.

But I'd come down the hall to find this.

I ran my hands down my face. "I can't repay you guys for this shit," I rasped, love for my family clogging my throat.

Vincent drew me into a one-armed hug. "This is what we do for family," he reminded me.

I swallowed thickly. "She lost her mucus plug last night," I told them. Silence fell over the room. "There's a huge possibility she's going to give birth today, and I don't know if I'm ready."

"You've got this, brother," Copper told me.

I ran my fingers through my hair. "I might need a babysitter for Randall. This is going to flip his world upside down. He's going to freak out—"

"Halen, stop," Logan told me. I blinked at him. "Vincent, Walker, and I will chill here at your place. We'll try to keep Randall's routine the same as much as possible. We can handle him. Focus on Genesis and the baby. The rest of us can handle everything else."

I nodded in thanks, drawing in a deep breath.

Thank fucking God for family.

I was right. Genesis was giving birth today. I held her hand in mine, brushing my other hand over her hair. She was being so fucking brave despite how terrified I knew she was.

"Is Randall going to be okay?" she asked me.

I smiled at her. "Yes, baby. He's going to be okay." At least, I hoped he was. "Vincent, Walker, and Logan are staying with him," I reminded her.

She leaned her head back, closing her eyes, a low moan of pain sliding past her lips. She was already at eight centimeters. When we got her to her appointment, she was at five.

Our baby was coming fast as fuck.

But Genesis was being brave as hell.

The time passed quickly. Before we knew it, Genesis was at ten centimeters, and she was pushing. She never cried, even though I got cursed a hell of a lot, but I took it in stride. I knew she was in pain, and I knew she was exhausted.

I just coaxed her through every push, encouraging her the best that I could. I didn't know what else to do for her.

Amber Hannah Anderson was born at twelve-fifteen that afternoon weighing four pounds on the dot. She wasn't completely developed yet and would need to spend some time in the hospital, but she was healthy.

I walked Randall through the steps of using the glove to touch his baby sister. "She looks like an alien," he whispered.

I snorted. "Give her some time, and she'll be a very pretty baby," I told him, though, in my eyes, Amber was already gorgeous, just like her mother. "You ready to go see your mom now?" I asked him once he'd gently touched his little sister for the first time.

He nodded. I grabbed his hand in mine, casting one more look at my daughter before I led him back to the other side of the fifth floor where Genesis was in her recovery room.

"How is she?" Genesis asked as soon as I stepped into the room.

"Sleeping," I told her. "Absolutely fucking precious."

"An alien," Randall corrected me.

Genesis rolled her lips into her mouth to keep from laughing. Randall climbed onto the bed and hugged Genesis. "Thank you, Mom."

"For?" she asked him, running her hand over his hair.

"For giving me a little sister like I wanted. She looks kind of strange right now, but Dad said she's going to be really pretty."

I ruffled his hair. Genesis pressed her lips to his head. "Yes, she is." Logan stepped into the room and handed Genesis a bouquet of flowers before leaning over and pressing a kiss to the top of her head.

"How are you feeling?" he asked her.

"Better now that I've had a nap and some food," she told him.

He grinned at her. "I think Skylar, Penny, Olivia, and Cassidy were freaking out more than you were."

Genesis laughed, looking over at me. She and I knew how much she had freaked out. Fuck, last night she'd had a panic attack when she lost her mucus plug. This morning, she had bawled when the doctor told her they had to deliver our little girl.

It hadn't been easy for her, but she didn't want everyone else knowing that. In her mind, if everyone else knew, it made the situation a lot scarier than it was. And honestly, once it was all said and done, she and I both realized we didn't really have anything to worry about.

Amber was going to be okay.

Randall jumped down from the bed, and I took his spot, curling my arm around Genesis, leaning down to softly kiss her. "You did so fucking good, babe."

She sighed. "I couldn't have done it without you."

"You're amazing," I told her with a grin.

She rolled her eyes, her cheeks burning. "So you keep telling me."

I kissed her again. "I'll always tell you," I reminded her "Because you are, and you deserve to hear it every fucking day."

She smiled at me. "I love you, Halen."

I kissed her again, this time making Randall groan in disgust. I laughed against Genesis's lips. "Seriously, Dad?"

Logan just laughed and led him from the room, saying something about going to get Randall some ice cream. Genesis smiled up at me. "Is she really going to be okay?" she asked, referring to our daughter.

I nodded. "She's going to do amazing," I assured her. "She's a fighter."

Genesis wrapped her arms around me. We sat like that for a while, just holding each other, but that was okay with me. I'd fought like hell to make this woman mine, and I knew that she and I could overcome anything, even something as terrifying as what we'd gone through today.

But I was right when I said Genesis was fucking amazing.

I wouldn't know what in the hell to do without her.

BOOK FIVE SNEEK PEEK
LOGAN

Link to Order: https://mybook.to/logan-tosmith

Walker walked outside, passing me a fresh beer before he dropped down onto the other picnic table. "Fucking ride was long as hell. I'm getting too old for this shit," he grumbled.

I snorted. "Says the man who volunteered for it," I retorted, giving him a pointed look. The last ride he'd just gone on with Grim had been completely voluntary. He needed extra hands at the exchange.

"Remind me of this shit when I volunteer again," Walker told me. He knew as well as I did that he would be up for a run the moment it was offered to him. Being ex-military, he missed the thrill he got while in danger. He missed having his life hanging in the balance.

Some of us got better with age. Others got worse.

Walker was one of those that got worse. I prayed for the woman he ever settled down with. She was going to have a hell of a man on her hands, that was for sure.

"Stop bitching," Vincent said as he walked outside, sitting next to Walker on the bench. "That ride was good for you. Helps keep all of us from bashing your head through a table when you get too pissy."

I barked out a laugh as Walker sent a kick against Vincent's shin with his steel-toed boot. The two of them were best friends – had served together overseas. And when Vincent came back home, he brought Walker with him, giving him a home here.

The sound of screeching tires suddenly reached my ears. Instantly, I dropped my beer, reaching for the gun in my cut. An old, beat-up, red Toyota slammed into the reinforced gates. Smoke billowed from the engine. The three of us waited for some kind of movement, but there was nothing.

"Cover me," I told the two men with me.

BOOK FOUR — HALEN

I stalked towards the car, my Glock in front of me as I made my way over to the wreck. A girl was drunkenly mumbling something, trying to get herself out of her seatbelt.

"You've got to be fucking shitting me," I swore. I didn't have the patience for bratty, drunk women. I liked my women obedient, and with one look at her fuming to herself, I knew she was going to be mouthy as fuck.

I wrenched the door open right as she got her seatbelt undone. She barely cast me a glance as she drunkenly pushed me aside and stumbled out of the car, her movements sloppy. I wrapped my hand around her upper arm before she face-planted on the ground.

She blinked a couple of times before running her eyes over me. "Are you going to call the cops?"

Walker barked out a laugh at that. I shook my head, steering her towards the side gate we'd come out of. "Vincent, Walker, deal with that piece of shit," I ordered.

"I'll get in touch with Copper," I heard Vincent say. I ignored him, working on trying to keep the drunk woman in my hold upright. She was piss drunk - way over the fucking legal limit. Hell, I didn't even think she was old enough to drink. She couldn't be a day over eighteen or nineteen. If she was, I'd be fucking surprised.

She stumbled, and I officially lost my patience. With a grunt, I swept her tiny body into my arms and strode towards the clubhouse, walking through the open door, heading towards the stairs off to the right.

"You got a name, little girl?" I asked her.

"Willow," she mumbled. She sloppily ran her hand over my cheek. "You're pretty."

I rolled my eyes. *Childish*. She was such a fucking child.

One I had zero fucking patience for.

"Got a last name, Willow?" I asked her, trying again.

"Jefferson," she mumbled, the single word heavily slurred. "But I am *nothing* like him."

Her last name meant trouble. There was only one family in this town with the last name Jefferson, and that was the mayor's family. We kept our distance from the mayor, did our best to stay off his radar.

That was going to go to shit now that his daughter had bashed her car into our fucking clubhouse gate – drunk, at that.

I placed her on my bed. She looked around her and fanned her face, her face scrunching up in displeasure. I looked at the ceiling, silently praying for someone to grant me some fucking patience. She was pushing every button she could.

"It's hot," she whined, her voice grating on my nerves. "Why is it so *hot*?"

"Because you're drunk," I told her. I looked back down at her. "Woman, what the fuck are you doing?!" I exploded, watching as she flung her top to the floor. She began yanking at her leggings. I threw my arms in the air in disbelief.

This shit wasn't seriously happening right now.

"I'm trying to *cool down*," she slurred. "It's *hot*."

Dear God, I needed help. For someone so small, she was curvy as fuck. But she was off-limits; she was the mayor's daughter. Not to mention, I didn't touch drunk women. It felt too much like rape, even if they consented.

Sometimes, what a drunk mind wanted, a sober one detested, and I wouldn't take a fucking chance.

I snatched a shirt out of my dresser and tossed it at her. "Put the shirt on," I ordered.

She huffed, glaring up at me. Her dark, curly hair was a mess and spread over my pillow. She looked too fucking enticing for her own damn good, and I needed her covered. Already, my cock was on hard just looking at her.

"It's *hot*. What don't you get?" she barked at me.

My patience snapped. I stormed over to the bed and snatched the shirt up before I leaned over her. I tightly gripped her chin in my hand, twisting her face back to look up at me when she looked away.

"I'm not in the habit of repeating myself," I growled at her. She swallowed thickly, sobering up a bit. "Put the fucking shirt on like I said, little one. Don't make me fucking have to tell you again."

I shoved the shirt at her chest and stood back up to my full height, watching as she obediently shrugged the shirt over her head.

Fucking finally.

"Get some rest," I ordered.

"Please don't leave me alone in here," she begged me, pouting her bottom lip. I closed my eyes and drew in a deep breath. "Pretty please?" she pleaded.

With a disgruntled sigh, I dropped into the chair in the corner of the room, lighting up a cigarette. She laid back down and pulled the blankets over her. She was silent for a while, but then, she started talking again, breaking the blissful peace I'd been enjoying.

I grunted. This girl was damn annoying.

"I had to drop out of college. It wasn't for me." *I did not care.* "Dad wanted me to pursue a degree in politics, go on to do great things, but I couldn't *focus*. All of my classes were so boring and dull, and without anyone to keep me in line like I had here at home, I kind of flunked," she confessed.

So, she was the kind of girl who needed someone to keep her in line. That was interesting.

I just kept my eyes steady on her. Her eyes were shut, her voice slowly going quieter the more she spoke. It wouldn't be long before she passed out.

"Dad flipped his shit when I came back home," she mumbled. "Got nowhere to go, now. Kicked me out. Said . . . worthless," she said, her voice going extremely soft as sleep tugged at her.

I continued watching her as her breathing evened out, soft snores leaving her lips. I shook my head and lit up another cigarette, unable to rip my eyes off her. Her makeup was smeared on her face, her hair a mess, and she looked troubled as hell.

But she was fucking beautiful. I'd give her that.

I leaned my head back, blowing smoke up at the ceiling. If there was one thing about men like me - we loved damsels in distress, and it was a plus when they needed someone to help keep them in line, keep them focused.

But Willow was untouchable - forbidden. The mayor's daughter and the outlaw biker could never have anything, not even a quick fuck.

I shook my head and stood up from the chair I'd been sitting in, going to find out what Vincent and Walker did with the car. She would be sleeping for a while. I had a good few hours before Willow would need anything.

And I needed to clear my head, and more importantly, drain my dick that was still hard. Looks like I was going on the search for a club girl first.

PLEASE LEAVE A REVIEW!

I would love to hear what you thought about the book!

Please hop over to Amazon, Goodreads, and/or BookBub and drop your review!

Every review, even the bad ones, are greatly appreciated!

Amazon: https://mybook.to/halen-tosmith

BookBub: Halen: Savage Crows MC Mother Charter Book 4 by T.O. Smith - BookBub

OTHER BOOKS BY T.O. SMITH

Find them on Amazon:

https://www.amazon.com/author/tosmith

Find them on her website:

https://tosmithbooks.com

FOLLOW T.O. SMITH

Facebook: https://www.facebook.com/authortosmith

Facebook group: https://www.facebook.com/groups/TOSmith

Instagram: https://www.instagram.com/authortosmith

Patreon: https://www.patreon.com/tiffwritesromance

Twitter: https://www.twitter.com/tiffwritesbooks

TikTok: https://www.tiktok.com/@tiffwritesromance

ABOUT THE AUTHOR

T.O. Smith believes in one thing - a happily ever after.

Her books are fast-paced and dive straight into the romance and the action. She doesn't do extensively drawn-out plots. Normally, within the first chapter, she's got you - hook, line, and sinker.

As a writer of various different genres of romance, a reader is almost guaranteed to find some kind of romance novel they'll enjoy on her page.

T.O. Smith can be found on Facebook, Instagram, Twitter, and now even TikTok! She loves interacting with all of her readers, so follow her!